Ever-After Island

Ever-After Island

by Elizabeth Starr Hill

E. P. Dutton / New York

Library of Congress Cataloging in Publication Data

Hill, Elizabeth Starr   Ever-after Island

SUMMARY: Two children accompany their scientist father
on an expedition to a remote island which they discover
to be inhabited by elves, mermaids, a wizard, and other
magical creatures.

[1. Fantasy]   I. Title
PZ7.H5514Ex   [Fic]   76-56859   ISBN: 0-525-29415-5

Published simultaneously in Canada by Clarke,
Irwin & Company Limited, Toronto and Vancouver

Editor: Ann Durell
Designer: Riki Levinson
Printed in the U.S.A.   First Edition
10 9 8 7 6 5 4 3 2 1

For Florence Longo
Like Gorth and Zender, she helps so much

Chapter

1

THE SCRATCHING SOUND woke Ryan up. It was coming through the wall, right near his head. At first he did not know what it was—or even where this room was, or why he was here.

He raised himself on one elbow and looked around sleepily, blinking. His father was still asleep in the other bed. A gray dawn light showed in the window, pearly with sea mist.

Then Ryan remembered. The summer of adventure was really beginning—had begun, in fact. Yesterday he and his sister Sara had arrived here from America with their father. After a long plane flight, they had taken a bus to this little inn on the northern coast of Europe. Today they were to join a group of other people and sail to a remote island—an island, so they had heard, which was like no place else.

"It was discovered by Dr. Moody Murk," their father, Professor Finney, had told them. "He's arranged the expedition. I've never met him, but I know his work."

"Does he study fish, the way you do?" Sara had asked.

"No, he's more interested in whole cultures, especially those nobody else knows much about. Years ago he wrote one book after another about tribal life in distant places. But he's quite old now. Lately—" Professor Finney hesitated.

Sensing a mystery, Ryan asked, "Lately what?"

"He's turned into sort of a hermit. Whenever anyone goes to see him, he says he needs to be alone—to read, read, read and think, think, think."

"What's he reading and thinking about?" Sara asked.

"No one knows. He's never been willing to tell what turn his thoughts have taken," Professor Finney said. "A year or so ago he hired a boat and a crew. It was said he was searching for an island. Last spring he found it—and brought back a couple of amazing things."

"What things?" Sara and Ryan asked together.

"A kind of mushroom no one's ever seen before—oddly striped, and folded like a tiny umbrella. *Very* strange. And even stranger, the bones of a little man-like creature, unknown to science."

"A monkey, you mean?" Ryan asked.

Sara gave him a superior smile. "Monkeys are not unknown to science, Ryan." She turned to their father. "Where is this island, Dad?"

Professor Finney pulled out a hand-drawn map. The island was only a dot, marked with an X. "Dr. Murk sent me this. He thinks there may be other rare forms of life there. And because of his past work, and the mushroom and bones he's found already, *Nature's*

Secrets magazine is putting up the money to explore the place further."

"Wow." Ryan rubbed his head so his thick yellow hair stood straight up. "And we're going to spend the whole *summer* there?"

Professor Finney nodded. "There'll be four other scientists besides Dr. Murk and me. And a reporter from *Nature's Secrets* is being sent along too, to take pictures and write about what we find."

"Will there be any kids except us?" Sara asked.

"I'm not sure. Exploring can be dangerous, as you know. And with a leader as odd as Dr. Murk—" he shrugged. "The others may leave their families at home."

The children's mother had died when Sara was two years old and Ryan only a baby. Rather than leave them behind with a housekeeper, Professor Finney took them with him whenever he could. Once they had spent two months on a boat while he studied the family life of the giant squid. Another year they had all camped on the ice near the North Pole, searching for Arctic minnows.

"If you've never met him, why did Dr. Murk choose you for this expedition, Dad?" Ryan said.

"Nobody knows more about fish than Dad does," Sara reminded him. Her eyes, the shiny hazel of wet leaves, flashed with pride. "He's *famous*. Aren't you, Dad?"

"In a small way," Professor Finney answered, his face pink and pleased. He looked quite young suddenly, and Ryan wished he had been the one to say something to please him. So often it was Sara who said just the right words instead.

"Dr. Murk must have read some of the papers you've written, Dad," she went on now. "He probably hopes you'll find a rare fish in the waters off the island."

"I suppose so. The real puzzle, though," Professor Finney pointed out, "is why Dr. Murk started searching for the island to begin with, and why he thinks there's anything more to be found there. He hasn't explained that."

"Well, no use trying to guess," Sara said, flipping back her brown braids. "It's foolish."

"You're right." Their father straightened his glasses briskly. "Guessing is a waste of time."

Ryan nodded, to be sociable. But he did not have a scientific mind, as his father and sister did. His was more like a runaway horse, always leaping off into questions and daydreams, not plodding from fact to fact.

So he kept wondering about what his father had said. How had Dr. Murk known that the island even existed? Why had he gone searching for it? And what —or who—lived on that dot of land in the ocean?

Now at dawn in the quiet inn, Ryan became wide awake. This was the very day they were to meet Dr. Murk and the other members of the expedition, and set off for the island!

As the scratching sound same again, Ryan remembered it was the signal he and Sara had agreed on—first one awake was to scratch on the wall between their two rooms. They had decided to get up early and go to the harbor, to see the boat that would take them out to sea.

Ryan tapped back softly to let Sara know he had heard. Then, grabbing his sneakers and sweater and jeans, he slipped out of the room without waking their father. Sara was waiting for him in the hall, already dressed. He threw his clothes on over his pajamas, and together they tiptoed silently downstairs and out into the misty hushed morning.

The street was empty, except for a black cat that ran across their path and vanished in an alley. It struck Ryan that black cats were supposed to be bad luck. He shivered a little, but did not mention his thought to Sara. She would laugh at him for believing in something like that.

"Which way do you suppose we should walk?" he whispered instead. They had arrived too late the night before to have any idea which direction the harbor was. Their father had said only that it was not far from the inn.

"As soon as the sun comes up, we can tell," Sara whispered back.

"How?"

Sara clucked as though his question were the dumbest one she had ever heard. "The boat has to be north of the town, since it's off the coast. When the sun rises, we can easily figure out where north is."

They waited as cold wisps of fog curled around corners and over the cobbled streets. Ryan's thoughts raced on, wondering what the boat would be like.

At last, a long rosy streak of light cut through the mist at the edge of the sky. "Okay, that's the east," Sara whispered. "This street should take us north, toward the coast."

Ryan followed her. Even in sneakers, their steps made a loud shushing sound as they hurried through the sleeping town.

Soon they saw a strip of rocky beach ahead, an old wharf, and the steely pale sea beyond. A fog bank floated above the water, and for a moment they thought no boat was there. Then the sun rose higher. The silvery moist air shifted and thinned. Suddenly they saw the outline of a large sailing ship riding in the harbor. It seemed unreal, as though scribbled across the morning sky.

"Why, it—it looks like a ghost ship," Ryan gasped. "The kind I've read about in books."

"Oh, those silly books you're always reading. The fog makes it look that way, that's all." Sara walked toward the wharf.

Ryan saw she was right. The ship looked more solid as the day brightened. He trailed after her out onto the wharf. They sat on the wooden pilings above the water and looked up at the tall masts. They could make out the slim form of someone on the rigging, a blue-jeaned figure—a sailor, Ryan thought.

The figure climbed down and dropped to the deck, and came over to the rail on their side. Ryan stared in surprise. It was not a boy, but a young woman, fresh-faced and red-cheeked from the sea air, her short red hair whipping about her head.

"Ahoy, mates," she called cheerfully. "Isn't this a fine ship? Have you ever seen a better one?" Her voice had a nice lilt to it.

"Never!" Ryan called back with a quick grin. "What's its name?"

"Has no name. What's yours?"

"Ryan Finney. This is my sister, Sara."

"Oh, the Finneys." She laughed. "We'll be seeing a lot of each other then. I'm Tracy Blair. I take pictures and write stories for *Nature's Secrets*. If you like, you can just call me Tracy."

She threw a rope ladder over the side, and clambered into a small dinghy beside the larger boat. "Coming ashore!" she called, rowing in.

She drew up at the dock in fine style, and tossed a rope to Ryan. He tied the boat fast to the dock.

Tracy hopped ashore. The fog had drawn away. The sun was very bright now. She squinted, watching a gull turn and dip in the air like an acrobat. "Must be fun to be a gull." She grinned, watching it. Then she turned a cartwheel herself, landing lightly between the two children.

"I think it must be fun to be a reporter," Ryan told her.

"Especially for *Nature's Secrets*," Sara put in. "That's one of my favorite magazines."

Tracy nodded. "It suits me. For a very special reason."

"Why?" Ryan asked quickly. Sara leaned past Tracy to frown at him for being nosy. Ryan paid no attention. He had learned long ago that if you try too hard to be polite, you may not find out much.

"Don't want to be bored. Not ever." Tracy looked at him with clear blue eyes. "The magazine sends me hunting mysteries, and I like that. I've written stories about what whales say to each other. And one about the music that plants like to listen to."

"What *do* they like to listen to?" Ryan asked, fascinated.

"Most prefer Bach, but some are crazy about Beethoven. I'm not sure why. Plants have their secrets too." She nodded toward the sailing ship. "Like our own Dr. Murk."

"Is he on the ship now?" Sara sounded excited in spite of herself.

"Sure he is. I talked with him yesterday, and again this morning."

"Well, what's he like?" The question burst out of Ryan.

Tracy shrugged. "Hard to say. So far, he hasn't really told me anything." She paused, then went on, "He has a big KEEP OUT sign on his cabin door, but I took a peek inside. The cabin was full of books. I've got a hunch they're a clue to something important."

"Did you look at their titles?" Ryan asked.

"I tried, but he has brown paper jackets on all of them, and I had no chance to open them. It's plain he doesn't want anyone to know what they are."

"Those books must be the ones Dad told us about—that Dr. Murk's been studying for so long," Sara said.

"Did I hear my name mentioned?" a cheerful voice asked from behind them. They all turned to see Professor Finney strolling toward them across the dock. He explained to Tracy, "These two tadpoles are mine, and they escaped this morning."

"Dad, this is Tracy," Ryan said eagerly. At Sara's sharp look, he insisted, "She said we could call her that. But you can call her Miss Blair, if you want to."

At this Tracy and Professor Finney both laughed. Something in the sound of their laughter made Ryan feel good. They were looking at each other as though pleased by what they saw. That gave Ryan a good feeling too. His father seemed lonely sometimes, but nobody could be lonely with Tracy around.

"I'd better take you kids off for breakfast." Professor Finney held out a hand each to Sara and Ryan. "Then we'll have our luggage brought on board. I understand Dr. Murk wants to set sail for the island before noon."

As he and Sara walked with their father through the narrow cobbled streets of the town, Ryan turned over in his mind what Tracy had said about Dr.

Murk's books: "I've got a hunch they're a clue to something important."

Those brown covered-up books. He would like to get a look inside one!

Just as Ryan thought that, the black cat ran across his path again.

Chapter

2

WHEN THE FINNEYS got back with their luggage, the ship was moored to the dock. A gangplank had been lowered to the dock from the ship. A small group of people were gathered near it; the other scientists, Ryan guessed. Members of the ship's crew milled around, getting the luggage on board.

Tracy waved; she was up on the rigging again.

"Do you suppose one of those men is Dr. Murk?" Ryan whispered to Sara.

"I don't see how any of them could be," she whispered back. "Dad said he was old." No man in sight looked more than middle-aged.

Professor Finney joined the waiting group near the gangplank, and introduced himself. "And this is my daughter Sara. And my son Ryan—"

Ryan tried to get the names and faces straight. There was Dr. Dank, a pale man with a discouraged smile. He described himself as a mushroom specialist. Professor Tendril, a vine and fern man, held out long thin fingers to shake hands with them. And a lively-looking couple named Mr. and Mrs. Gust explained that they were experts on weather and tides.

The Gusts had their son with them, a chubby little boy named Punky. His mother said he and the Finneys were the only children going on the trip.

Ryan sighed as he heard this. It was hard to imagine liking a kid named Punky, and this one seemed especially unlovable. He had a loud voice, and kept asking *why* all the time. "Why do we have to walk up that plank? Why can't we eat lunch before we go? Why is that cat watching us like that?"

Ryan glanced up, startled. The black cat sat on the railing of the ship above them, its yellow eyes fixed on them.

"Maybe it's the ship's mascot," Mrs. Gust said. "Remember, in your pirate book it told about mascots. It said they were thought to have magic powers."

"To do what?" Punky asked.

"Well, to protect the ship while the mascot is on board. The legend is that if a mascot misses a voyage, the ship will be lost. Wasn't that it?" She smiled. "I've forgotten now."

Perhaps the mention of pirates put the thought in his head, or maybe he would soon have noticed it anyway. But Ryan found himself staring at the sailors who were loading the luggage, and thinking that they looked like fierce men.

One, the tallest of them, seemed the most sinister. He carried a dagger between his teeth, wore a single earring, and had a bandanna tied around his head. His brows were black and threatening as thunder. A large green parrot was perched on his shoulder.

Ryan swallowed. It occurred to him that the man looked exactly like a bold, tough pirate, the kind who showed no mercy.

"All aboard!" this man shouted from the deck. He had taken the dagger from his mouth and was brandishing it in the air. "I'm the captain of this ship, and I tell ye to board now!"

Ryan obeyed, like everyone else, but he felt nervous as he followed his father and Sara up the gangplank. The phrase "walking the plank" came into his mind. He hated walking toward the fierce captain who loomed above them, scowling, the dagger between his teeth again. The presence of the black cat did not help him much, either. He tried to avoid its yellow eyes.

As he neared the top of the gangplank, a wild screech nearly made him jump out of his skin. Then he realized it was just the parrot. "Dr. Murk!" the bird squawked, looking at someone across the deck. "Murk! Murk! Murk!"

An old man walked toward them, dressed as a seaman, in worn jeans and a threadbare shirt. His white hair drifted around his head like puffs of dandelion. He did not look rough or dangerous, like the crew. His eyes were gentle and had a faraway expression, as though his mind were on something not to be shared.

"So these are the brave ones who are coming with me to Ever-After Island," he said. Then he murmured to himself, "I wonder how it will all end?"

"Brave! Brave!" shrilled the parrot. "End!"

The black cat leaped from the railing with a howl, sprinted across the deck, and disappeared down a stairway. A chill ran through Ryan like ice water through a straw. It seemed to him that the howl had sounded like a wicked laugh.

Punky asked, "Why is it called Ever-After Island?"

"And why do you call us brave ones?" Sara asked, her voice quivering a little.

"Yeah, why?" Punky echoed loudly.

Dr. Murk passed a hand across his eyes. "I'm sorry. I'm not used to people. I say the wrong things."

Ryan remembered their father had told them Dr. Murk had become almost a hermit. He felt sorry for the old man. It must be hard to take charge of an expedition like this, after being alone so much, for so many years.

Dr. Murk went on, "It's my private name for the island. A—a joke, really. And as for needing to be brave—well, as long as you all obey the rules, there may not be much danger."

"What rules?" several people asked.

"Put to sea! Put to sea!" the parrot screeched.

"Yes, it's time for us to cast off," Dr. Murk said. "As soon as we're underway, I'll explain what I mean." His tone was stronger now, and his gaze less distant. Ryan thought he might not make a bad leader after all.

The black-browed captain ordered his crew to take their positions. Tracy climbed down from the rigging. With a smile that looked slightly shy, she came to stand near Professor Finney at the rail. Ryan thought she was blushing, but it might have been sunburn.

In a few minutes, the ship began to move. Gulls cried overhead, following it, hoping for scraps of food. The sparkling water widened between the ship and the dock, and the little town began to fade in the distance.

"We should reach the island late this afternoon," Dr. Murk announced, his white hair streaming in the fresh wind.

"I do hope there'll be enough light to see mushrooms," Dr. Dank sighed, with his discouraged downward smile.

"Why do you like mushrooms?" Punky asked him.

"They're the only perfect objects in the world," Dr. Dank told him seriously.

This was typical of scientists, Ryan thought. They took such a narrow view. He was sure his father would say the same thing about fish.

Dr. Murk went on, "We'll probably be able to get our tents set up by dark. There's a nice level spot for them, right near the beach."

Ryan felt a thrill of anticipation. He enjoyed sleeping in a tent, hearing the songs of frogs and insects, and listening to birds warble off to sleep. He liked the soft moistness of summer night air, the glimmer of starshine, and the first piercing calls of the birds in the morning. Best of all, he liked waking up to find himself already outdoors, with a whole new place to discover.

"Let's go below, and I'll tell you about the island," Dr. Murk said. "The crew has lunch ready for us."

Tracy and the Finneys, Dr. Dank, Professor Tendril, and finally the three Gusts, trailed Dr. Murk down a ladder-like stairway. He led them to the ship's galley, where several of the scowling crew were waiting for them.

A huge pot of stew bubbled on the black iron stove. The dark-browed captain himself, with the parrot on his shoulder, was stirring it. It smelled delicious, but Ryan had uncomfortable thoughts about it. With a cook like that, a pinch of arsenic in the salt seemed likely.

Dr. Murk and the other scientists, and Tracy and the children, sat together around a big wooden table. The captain plopped steaming bowls of stew and thick crackers before them, but did not sit down. Neither did any of the other sailors. They just walked around, looking mean, or leaned against the walls.

Dr. Murk began eating right away, which made Ryan feel better. Since the old scientist trusted the stew, he decided to, too. He forked into it hungrily. It tasted as great as it smelled.

"Why aren't those sailors eating with us?" Punky asked in his loud voice.

Dr. Murk glanced vaguely at the crewmen. "Oh, they don't need to eat. That is, they don't care to. Not right now."

"Don't eat," the parrot screeched. "Don't, don't, don't."

Dr. Murk's answer seemed odd to Ryan. He saw from Tracy's face that she thought so too; her eyebrows curved up questioningly. All the sailors Ryan had ever known—and because of his father's work, he had known many—had been early and hearty eaters.

"You mean they eat someplace else?" Punky persisted.

Dr. Murk looked helpless and apologetic. He muttered the same words he had spoken before: "I'm not used to people. I say the wrong things."

Ryan looked at Tracy. She gave a small puzzled shrug. He understood now why she had learned little in talking to Dr. Murk; the man talked in riddles.

Ryan thought of the mysterious books, jacketed in brown paper, that she had seen in the scientist's cabin. Again he longed to get a look at them.

Suppose he were to slip away from the table right now. While Dr. Murk ate stew and told his plans for the expedition, his cabin would be empty. Nearly everybody on the ship was right here in the galley. The few other crew members must be busy keeping the ship moving, and on course.

If he could just find the right cabin—

"You all know of the discoveries I've made on the island so far," Dr. Murk was saying. He repeated the facts about the mushrooms and the little bones. As he spoke, Ryan started to slide out of his chair carefully, hoping no one would notice.

Punky's chubby face turned toward him. Ryan froze, knowing it was only a matter of seconds before

17

the kid would say, "Why are you getting up from the table?"

"I've made drawings of plant life that I have reason to believe may exist on the island," Dr. Murk said. "Unusual pumpkins. And some absolutely fantastic vines."

"Oh?" Professor Tendril's eyelids fluttered with interest. "What kind?"

"Probably a gigantic form of bean. I didn't see any myself, but I'm sure you'll keep looking."

"Of course," Professor Tendril assured him.

To Professor Finney, Dr. Murk added, "And for you, I have a drawing of a *very* rare fish that may live in the waters around the island. I am most anxious for you to find it, if you can."

"Naturally, I'll do my best," Professor Finney replied. "What is this fish, and why do you think it's there?"

A guarded look came over the old man's face. "It's not an ordinary fish. It has never been studied before, so I have almost no information about it."

"Yet you've made a drawing of it?" Professor Finney asked in surprise.

"It may not be an exact likeness."

"You haven't told us what your reason is for believing it exists," Professor Tendril said. "Or the giant vines either. Or the pumpkins."

Dr. Murk looked more guarded than ever; crafty, almost. "I have sources which I will not reveal," he said firmly.

18

Ryan thought of the books again. He finished the last of his stew, and decided again to get away. If Punky asked why he was leaving, he could say he had to go to the bathroom.

But Dr. Murk's next words changed his mind. "You three children be sure to listen carefully now." The old scientist looked at each of them in turn. "I promised to give you some rules for personal safety. These rules apply to each one of us. None of us can afford to be careless."

Like the others, Ryan sat quite still, his attention riveted. He had a creepy, crawly feeling. Dr. Murk went on solemnly, *"There is the possibility of grave danger on the island—perhaps worse than any of us can imagine."*

Chapter
3

DR. MURK CONTINUED, "The weather on the island is hard to predict. Sudden storms blow up, and there can be fearsome tides." He added to Mr. and Mrs. Gust, "You'll find that interesting."

"Fascinating." Mr. Gust nodded with pleasure, and Mrs. Gust clapped her hands in happy expectation.

"We will have several rowboats with us, which Dr. Finney and others of you will need in your work. But because of the weather hazards, *no one must stay out in a boat if any sign of bad weather develops.* Get ashore as quickly as possible, and take cover."

The old scientist glanced around the table. "Is that clear?"

Grownups and children all nodded or murmured in agreement. Ryan wondered why Dr. Murk thought it necessary to warn them of that. Any fool knew enough to come in from a storm at sea.

"But the greatest danger may not be the weather." Dr. Murk spoke slowly and seriously, as though to make them realize the importance of every word. "There is a native population on the island. They live behind a high wall, surrounded by a forest. I have never seen them."

"Why do you think they're a danger, then?" Tracy asked.

"Once when I was walking in the forest, I was pelted with stones from behind that wall. The stones bruised my shoulder badly. Clearly, someone was trying to get rid of me. And didn't mind hurting me to do it."

Ryan's heart thumped. Sara's face looked pale and scared. Punky was silent for a change, listening with round eyes.

Dr. Dank put in, "Island folk can be touchy when people intrude on their territory. Once I was set upon by cannibals on an island off South America."

"How awful." Professor Tendril twined his long hands together in agitation. "How did you escape?"

"Talked them into eating mushrooms I knew were poisonous. Wiped out the whole tribe before they could eat me," Dr. Dank said with satisfaction, his gloomy face brighter than usual.

"We might not escape as easily from the natives on Ever-After Island," Dr. Murk remarked. "So one of the most important rules of this expedition is—*stay away from that wall!* Don't go deep into the forest. There'll be plenty to see and do around the shore."

He mentioned some other, minor rules about the care of tents and equipment. Ryan barely listened. His imagination was completely captured by the thought of those natives, and their unknown village in the heart of the island. Did they live in thatched huts? he wondered. Or were they more primitive? Cave dwellers, perhaps? Did they ever stray out from their walled enclosure?

What connection was there, if any, between them and the bones Dr. Murk had found?

Tracy's gaze met his. He felt that her mind, too, was teeming with questions. But Dr. Murk and the other scientists were off on a conversation about tent pegs and campfire control.

"May I go up on deck and feed my crackers to the sea gulls?" Sara asked Dr. Murk politely. "I don't care for any more to eat."

"Yes. Yes, of course," he answered, absently.

She glanced at her father. Professor Finney nodded.

Sara gathered her crackers carefully and pushed out from the table. Punky, too, jumped up, seized a handful of crackers, and asked loudly, "Why can't I feed the gulls too?"

"You can, I guess," Sara told him without enthusiasm.

"Of course." Punky's mother smiled. "Have a good time. Don't fall overboard."

"I never do." Punky lifted his chubby chin and stalked off after Sara.

Ryan had eaten his crackers already, but he saw the chance to get away. He left the galley with the others, then let them get ahead of him. As they went up on deck, he turned quickly into an empty corridor.

He had walked only a few yards when he came to a closed door. It bore a large handwritten sign: KEEP OUT. Suddenly Ryan remembered what Tracy had said about the sign on Dr. Murk's door. This, then, must be his cabin—and inside, perhaps a clue to the mysteries of Ever-After Island.

Ryan stood still outside the door, getting up courage. Now that the moment was at hand, he felt very nervous about going into Dr. Murk's private room. What if a member of the crew were tidying up in there? Worse yet, what if the old scientist himself left the lunch table and caught him?

Still, Ryan told himself, there probably never would be a better time than this. The idea of giving up, of not finding out what was in the books, did not even occur to him.

Tight tingles of nervousness passed through his stomach and chest. His clenched fists were clammy. But he drew a long breath and rapped on the door. If one of the sailors were inside, he would say he had gotten lost and was looking for his sister.

There was no answer to his knock. Slowly and cautiously Ryan opened the door, darted in and closed it behind him.

He found himself in a small darkish room. The only light came from the round porthole on the far wall. The glass was dirty, caked with salt spray. It took a few seconds for his eyes to adjust to the dimness. Then he saw a bunk, a table and chair—and books.

Shelves and boxes of books. Books of every size, covered with brown paper, nothing to show what they were about.

His heart thudding, Ryan listened to the creaking of the ship and the muted cries of the gulls. He could hear nothing else, no one coming.

He crossed the cabin swiftly, pulled a book from a shelf, and opened it.

What had he expected? He did not know, had had no expectaton. Yet as he read a few lines on the page before him, he was astonished and bewildered. "Far, far from land, where the waters are as blue as the petals of the cornflower and as clear as glass, there, where no anchor can reach the bottom live the mer-people."

Ryan knew this story. It was "The Little Mermaid" by Hans Christian Andersen, one of his favorite writers. But what was it doing here? It was a child's story, a fairy tale. Why the brown jacket, as though it contained an important secret?

He put the book down and opened another, to a page with a colored picture on it. The picture showed a boy staring upward at an enormous vine. The words beneath it read, "So Jack jumped up and dressed himself and went to the window. And what do you think he saw? Why, the beans his mother had thrown out of the window into the garden had sprung up into a big beanstalk, which went up and up until it reached the sky."

Ryan went over this again, hardly believing he could have got it right the first time. Dr. Murk, studying "Jack and the Beanstalk"? Was the old man crazy, then? Were they in the clutches of a madman, sailing off into nowhere?

Feverishly Ryan grabbed a third book. He read, "And the fish said to him, 'Listen, fisherman, I beg of you, let me live. I am not a real fish; I am an enchanted Prince.'"

Ryan's hands began to tremble. He leafed through this whole book. It was Grimm's fairy tales. Unsteadily he stuck it back on its shelf, feeling terribly mixed up. Surely, surely there must be some mistake. There must be something in this cabin that explained Dr. Murk's theories, something he thought was true and worth learning more about.

Ryan knew he dared not stay in here too long. The sooner he got out, the better. Lunch in the galley was likely to break up any minute. But he could not resist trying one more book, just one. He chose it from a box, and opened it with a sense of last, feeble hope.

Words wobbled to him from the page, in curly letters trimmed with flowers: "'Come to the island where my kingdom is,' the Prince begged her. 'We will marry and live happily ever after.'"

Ever after. Ever-After Island.

Ryan dropped the book back into its box. The ship swayed. He was dizzy, and wondered if he was going to be sick to his stomach. He crossed to the door, opened it a crack, and peered out. The corridor was still empty. He reeled out into it and made his way to the stairs that led up to the deck.

On deck in the fresh air, everything seemed better. Ryan looked around in relief. The bright sunlight danced off the water. Noisy gulls grabbed bits of crackers as Sara and Punky threw them. Grownups stood around talking. It seemed safe up here, normal. His father was laughing with Tracy. Dr. Murk chatted with the other scientists.

The captain, with his parrot, was watching Sara and Punky. He did not look fierce or evil now. In fact Ryan imagined there was a sadness about him, a sort of wistfulness.

Perhaps Sara noticed it too. She turned, the last piece of cracker in her hand, and smiled uncertainly into the black-browed captain's face. "May I speak to your parrot?"

He nodded, not unkindly.

Always polite, Sara asked the bird, "Would you care for a cracker?"

"Don't eat!" it screeched; and Ryan fancied this, too, was sad. "Don't eat at all!"

"Oh!" Again Sara gave her uncertain little smile. "I see." She threw the last crumb to the gulls.

Ryan walked away from the group and leaned against the rail. The black cat was perched on it again, a short distance away. He paid no attention to it, nor it to him.

Too much had happened in this day. Ryan was worn out, tired of thinking, tired of trying to make sense of things. The plane flight the day before had been long. He had been up very late last night, and had gotten up early this morning. His brains felt fogged in with weariness and puzzlement.

The ship swayed, back and forth, back and forth. Scarcely able to keep his eyes open, Ryan looked around for a spot to lie down. He saw a heavy coil of rope on the deck. Gratefully he curled up on it. It had a good rough shape, comfortable around him. He sank into sleep, letting go of all his troubled thoughts.

When he next awoke, the sun was lower in the sky, but not very much. The ship was still moving along. There seemed no reason to wake up completely yet. He shifted, and drifted, and dozed.

The books in Dr. Murk's cabin were still in his mind, but not as a problem now. Instead, he remembered reading fairy tales himself, and loving them. He had always wished the world could be more like a fairy tale. Why, he had always wondered, did grownups have to go to work, or pay bills, or do the dishes? Why couldn't they just stumble across a money tree, or get some help from a friendly elf?

Why did kids have to go to school? Clean their rooms? Wear rubbers? It would be so much more fun to pop a mean witch into an oven, or ride a magic carpet, or turn your least favorite teacher into a turnip.

When he was younger, it had seemed to him that there must be some place where make-believe came true. But finally he had pretty much given up on it. Sometimes it seemed that the older you got, the more boring everything was supposed to be. You put the garbage out and fed the dog. You went from first grade to second grade, second to third. With any luck, it went on like that. But where was the excitement?

What was it Tracy had said? "Don't want to be bored. Not ever."

Me either, Ryan thought. He nestled into the coarse rope and fell asleep again.

When he awakened again, the light was softer and rosier against his eyelids. He looked up and saw a gilded throw of sunset clouds across the blue sky. It was a fair and lovely late afternoon. The motion of the ship was different. They seemed to be going slower.

But what had really wakened him, he realized, was a sweet bell-like voice. It seemed to be singing softly from somewhere in the sea below. Listening carefully, Ryan could just make out the words of the song:

> "Once I longed for a beautiful shell.
> It shone at me from the ocean floor.
> When I dove to get it, it moved away,
> And I never look anymore.

> "I wanted to taste a delicate weed.
> They said it grew near a distant land.
> I swam to find it, but soon gave up,
> And ate something near at hand.

"I met a Prince from the landings' world.
We fell in love—and I love him still.
The Wizard thinks I will soon forget,
But I never ever will. . . ."

The last verse was sung so forlornly that Ryan called out quickly, without thinking, "I'm so sorry. Can I do anything?"

There was a startled silence. Ryan rolled out of his rope and looked down at the water through the ship's railing. He saw a large gleaming fishtail flip just above the surface, then sink out of sight. There was a rock near it. In a second, the ship had moved on. Ryan could not be certain of what he had really seen.

The bell-like voice did not sing anymore. Could he have imagined it? Might it have been a dream? He was not sure. He walked around the deck and met Sara. She said, "I was just coming to wake you up."

"Did you hear someone singing?" he asked her.

"Singing? No. But we've all been talking. Look." She pointed. "We're almost there. There's Ever-After Island!"

Ryan ran toward the prow of the ship where the others were clustered at the rail, their shadows long across the deck. He passed the captain, who was standing alone with his parrot on his shoulder.

So eager was Ryan to see the island that although he noticed something strange, he did not think it strange until later.

The captain cast no shadow.

Chapter
4

RYAN AND SARA AND PUNKY stood together in the prow of the ship. They looked delightedly at the island's wide rocky beach and tall swaying trees, coming closer every second. In the clear low sunshine, every leaf seemed shot through with jewel-like greens and yellows. Each little hollow in the rocks was a cup of darkness. Even the grains of sand made a texture that you could see, a lovely golden roughness.

On such fine days, and especially at this hour in the last of the afternoon, Ryan sometimes felt that the world was just too beautiful to be the same old world. It seemed to have been polished up into something else; the beauty itself gave a strangeness to everything.

Tracy must have felt the same way. He heard her voice, full of wonder, saying, "And we'll be here for months."

Ryan turned impulsively to Sara. "Won't it be great?"

She nodded, her eyes shining. "I'm going to study and classify seaweed."

"Good." Their father nodded approvingly. "No use wasting the summer."

"And Punky's going to work on his shell collection, aren't you, dear?" Mrs. Gust patted Punky's blond cowlick. "Such a worthwhile project."

"Wish I didn't have to," Punky grumbled.

Ryan glanced down at him with sympathy. Here was something, at least, that he and the smaller boy had in common. Ryan hated worthwhile projects. He hated the whole idea of not wasting time. He thought that was the best way to spend it—carelessly and happily, like birthday money. What was better than a day you could not account for? But he kept these thoughts to himself.

The ship had almost reached a ramshackle dock that jutted out into the water. "I built that when I was here last," Dr. Murk said. "It'll make it easier to unload the tents and luggage."

The unloading went quickly, with the sailors working hard. In just a little while, rowboats had been lowered and tied to the dock. The passengers and equipment were on shore. And the black-browed captain and his crew returned to the ship and pulled up the gangplank.

"Are they leaving us here?" Mrs. Gust asked with concern.

"Yes, they have to keep sailing," Dr. Murk said. "But don't worry. I gave them a radio so we can signal them in case of an emergency. They'll come back if we need them."

"Oh, good. . . . Come on, Punky. You can help us set up the tents."

31

The glowing ball of sun still hung in the sky. It was cool and pleasant on the dock. "Let's stay to watch the ship go," Ryan suggested to Sara.

The others bustled around at the edge of the woods, setting up camp. Sara and Ryan alone watched the ship sail off on the ebbing tide, followed by gulls. Ryan noticed the black cat was no longer on the rail. He wondered if it had come ashore.

It was at that instant that the ship disappeared.

Sara gasped. Ryan blinked and rubbed his eyes. But it had vanished. It was gone as though it had never been. Above the spot where they had last seen it, the gulls flew in confused broken patterns. It seemed they, too, had trouble believing their eyes.

Sara was the first to speak. "There's no mist," she said faintly.

"No." Ryan could see the gulls' wings perfectly plainly, and this horrified him. No mist to hide the ship, the day still fine and fair.

"But what is it, then?" Sara turned to Ryan with a look of panic. "What's happened?"

Her panic deepened Ryan's horror. Memories struck him, each one important now. The ghostly look of the ship this morning. The way none of the sailors—not even the parrot—would eat anything. The fact that the captain and the parrot had cast no shadow, when other shadows were long across the deck.

The other sailors had been busy elsewhere then, but maybe it was the same with them—*as with all ghosts!*

For what could these things mean, Ryan asked himself in fear and bewilderment, except that it really *was* a ghost ship? A pirate vessel, lost at sea and doomed to keep sailing forever.

Suddenly he felt sure of it. There were many legends about such ships and their ghostly crews. He had often read and heard about them. Old sailors he had known swore the legends were true.

Once Ryan had believed in them, along with the other stories. What if his younger self had been right, after all? What if life was sometimes, in some places, magical—the way children always imagined it should be, and most grownups denied it ever was?

Usually Ryan thought of magic as being splendid and joyful. Now he saw it could be frightening too. Suppose the ghost ship never returned to the island. No one could manage a trip over so many miles of open sea, in only a rowboat. They would never get back to the mainland without that ship.

Could you count on ghosts?

Ryan longed to talk to Tracy, to share his fears and questions with her. She would never laugh at him. He was sure of it. She would help him get his jumbled, excited thoughts straightened out.

"Well?"

He realized his sister was still waiting for him to answer. "Sara, lots of people believe in ghost ships," he began hesitantly.

"Oh, there you go again, just like this morning."

33

He did not reply. It was no use. If you could not prove something to Sara, it was hard to get her to even consider it.

"Maybe we were absentminded for a minute." She looked out at the place where the ship had disappeared. "It must have turned and gone around the island."

"No, it didn't. I'm sure not. Look at the gulls. They're still milling around, wondering what happened."

"But it must have. There's no other reasonable explanation."

Ryan felt impatient. If only he could talk to Tracy instead of Sara. Tracy was with everybody else over near the woods, setting up the tents. Maybe later, around the campfire, he would be able to speak to her without anyone else hearing.

She noticed him looking in her direction, and waved. "Hey, you two, how about lending a hand? As soon as the tents are squared away, we can eat dinner."

"Coming," Sara called. To Ryan she added crossly, "I wish you'd try to figure things out scientifically."

"I *am* trying. I just come up with different answers from the ones you get."

At the campsite, Ryan learned he was to share a tent with Punky, which was depressing. Sara would share one with Tracy, Mr. and Mrs. Gust would be together, and Dr. Dank with Professor Tendril. Professor Finney would be alone with his tanks. Dr. Murk had a tent to himself too—so he could keep his books a secret, Ryan supposed.

Pounding a tent peg into the ground, Ryan thought about those books, but his thoughts led nowhere. He thought about the ship, but that was upsetting. He tried to put it out of his mind. Then, he got wondering instead about the natives behind the stone wall, in the middle of the forest.

He squatted on his heels and stared at the dimming trees near the beach. It was dusk now. The trees seemed bluish and dark in the twilit air. That was the edge of the forest. Further in, where they had been warned not to go, it would be darker still. He pictured the dense tall woods in there, the high stone wall, and behind it—what?

Again he wondered if the natives ever came out from behind the wall. Did they know the expedition had landed? Might they, even now, be watching them?

As he thought this, two glowing spots of light caught his attention. They seemed to come from a tree branch just inside the woods. There was something vaguely familiar about the set of them. With an eerie chill, he realized they looked like yellow eyes, eyes he had seen sometime before.

Or did they? Could they be fireflies? No, fireflies went on and off. Or stars shining through the tree branches? They seemed bigger than that, and it was still early for stars.

"I'm hungry," Punky's loud voice told the world.

He was not far from Ryan, and had also been pounding in tent pegs. This tent, the nearest to the shore, was the one they were to share. "When are we going to eat dinner?"

"Right away," Dr. Murk called. "Professor Finney, will you make a campfire?"

"Punky," Ryan whispered hoarsely, "do you see a pair of eyes over there?"

"What kind of eyes?"

"*Any* kind of eyes. Those yellow spots."

"Where?"

"Will you stop shouting? Right over there in the trees." But now the spots of light were gone. Ryan said weakly, "I think someone was watching us."

"Who?"

"How do I know who?" Yet the yellow eyes had seemed familiar.

Then he remembered the black cat.

"Everybody ready for dinner?" Dr. Murk called genially. "We'll have to eat a lot of dried and canned food in the weeks ahead, but tonight we have steaks."

Steaks, cooked on a fire! Ryan realized how hungry he was. The stew had been long ago. He jumped up and headed over to where his father was making the fire.

"Dr. Dank, is it too dark for you to find some mushrooms?" Dr. Murk asked. "They'd be good with steak."

"Nothing poisonous, you know," Professor Tendril tittered.

"I'll try." Taking his mushroom-collecting basket, Dr. Dank walked off into the woods. Everyone else gathered around the campfire. Dr. Murk threw the steaks on.

Within minutes Dr. Dank returned, swinging his basket breathlessly. "Look! Look what I found!"

He held up the largest mushroom Ryan had ever seen, and surely the oddest. One edge of it turned up; it looked less like a toadstool than like a very modern miniature chair. Further, its color was a strong, stylish pink.

As everyone gaped at this, Dr. Dank pulled out another. Brownish, with a flat irregular top, it resembled a little free-form table.

Tracy said exactly what Ryan was thinking: "They look like furniture for elves."

Dr. Murk turned and glanced at her sharply, but said nothing.

"Here's another. This seems much like the one you found when you were here before, Dr. Murk." Dr. Dank produced a blue and purple striped mushroom which he carefully folded and unfolded, just like a toy umbrella.

"I'm not eating any of those," Punky told everybody.

"Of course not. These are valuable specimens. And I'm not through yet." Triumphantly, Dr. Dank pulled the last of his finds from the basket. Looking at it, Ryan felt his scalp prickle. It was a bright green shoe, about as big as his little finger, and it came to a long point at the toe. If ever something looked like a shoe for an elf, this was it.

"My goodness." Professor Tendril touched the little shoe. "The native children must play with dolls."

It was an explanation. But Ryan thought it was not the right one.

Tracy got out flashbulbs and took pictures of the mushrooms and the shoe. Then Dr. Dank stowed his discoveries in his tent and rejoined the others at the campfire. Dr. Murk opened cans of beans to have with the steaks. Darkness slowly inked out the sky and woods and beach. Everyone ate and laughed and talked, in the flickering orange circle of firelight.

Somewhere a nightingale sang. Two owls swooped overhead, then were gone. A cricket chirped, "Jiminy? Jiminy?" and a chorus of frogs croaked rhythmically.

Ryan listened to these night sounds, enjoying them, and the good food, and the warm fire in the cool evening. He was wedged between Sara and Punky in the circle. With Sara near enough to notice his manners, he tried not to pile too many beans on his fork, or to eat the steak too fast. Punky was less restrained; he simply cut the meat into strips and stuffed it into his mouth with his fingers.

Ryan had hoped to speak privately with Tracy. But she was across the campfire from him, talking to his father. It seemed to Ryan that their faces looked young and very alive, their eyes happy. Tracy's red hair caught the shine of the fire, and her cheeks were flushed by it—or maybe she was blushing again.

Mrs. Gust's breezy voice broke through his reverie: "Punky looks sleepy. Shall we get the kids into their sleeping bags?"

Annoyed, Ryan told her, "Nobody has to get me into mine, thanks. And I'm not sleepy yet."

"Neither am I." Sara was still cutting her steak into neat pieces and chewing it well. "It's so nice here by the fire."

Protesting, Punky was dragged off to the tent, but the Finneys were allowed to stay.

"I'll get my guitar," Tracy said; and she did. In her lilting, cheerful voice, she sang songs that most of them knew. Soon nearly everybody was joining in. They sang until the fire burned low, and a thin moon rose over the sea.

At last, yawning, they made sure the fire was out, and straggled off to the tents. Ryan found Punky snoring loudly. Even that noise, though, could not keep him awake for longer than it took to get into his pajamas and sleeping bag.

He was awakened in the middle of the night by a high piping voice. It was neither bird nor cricket nor frog, but it was not quite human, either. "Let's try this tent first," it said.

"I wish you wouldn't insist on going inside the tents." The other voice had the same inhuman piping quality. "It's *so* dangerous."

"You can hear this one snoring," the first voice pointed out. "Nobody wakes up easily from a sound sleep like that."

"How do you know? You don't know anything about humans."

"I know more than you think. My great-grandfather lived in the garden of a human for years and years. He died in a very dry summer, when no mushrooms grew. My grandfather told me about it."

"It's not worth taking the risk, for just a shoe. They might catch us and pickle us, or whatever they do."

"It's *my* shoe, and my foot is cold. I'm going to find it, if it takes all night."

Ryan clutched the top edge of his sleeping bag, staring at the tent flap. It opened at the bottom. In came two tiny creatures, only about a foot tall. Each carried a white mushroom that shone like a lamp in the darkness.

Chapter
5

THEY WERE almost like tiny men, except that their ears were pointed and their noses and bellies comically large. They were dressed entirely in leafy green with peaked caps, and wore pointed shoes exactly like the one Dr. Dank had found in the woods.

That is, one did. The other, who was stouter and seemed the older of the two, had one bare foot, and a determined attitude. He saw Punky's open suitcase, stuck his mushroom lamp near it on the ground, and began riffling through the suitcase without even glancing around the rest of the tent.

The other looked more timid. He almost cowered under his mushroom, his eyes fixed on Punky's snoring face. They both seemed convinced that Punky was the only person present. They had not noticed Ryan, who lay stiff and tense, not moving a muscle.

Wildly, Ryan told himself they must be wind-up toys of some kind. They would run down in a minute, like the demonstration models salesmen started on the sidewalk. But he knew it wasn't so. The timid face, brightly lighted by his mushroom, had lined flesh, and quirky brows, and worried eyes. The little hands, rummaging through Punky's suitcase, were as quick and skillful as human hands.

They were real. Real elves. Ryan had seen hundreds of pictures in his storybooks that made him sure he was right.

He remembered those tiny bones Dr. Murk had found; elf bones, they must have been. And it occurred to him Dr. Murk might have suspected that Ever-After Island was a magic place. He had studied the fairy tales, gone searching for the island, called it by that name—

As these thoughts flashed through Ryan's mind, the stout elf finished his quest through Punky's suitcase. "It's not in there," he piped irritably, "and my toes are curling with cold."

Ryan looked at his toes. It was true. He had very long ones—so that was why they wore such pointy shoes!—and they were curled upward, rather like skis. It was a pathetic sight.

On impulse, Ryan said, "It's in Dr. Dank's tent. So is some of your furniture, I think."

He spoke softly, so as not to frighten them or wake Punky. Yet both elves leaped several inches into the air. Their faces turned as pale as their mushrooms. The more timid one scrambled to get out of the tent. In his panic, he only got tangled in the tent flap.

"Don't be scared," Ryan whispered. "I won't hurt you."

This seemed to calm them slightly. "But you're a

42

scientist, aren't you?" the stouter one asked. "Picking up whatever—and whoever—you can?"

"Me?" Ryan laughed. "No, I'm only a boy."

"A boy!" The timid elf disentangled himself from the tent flap, and gaped at Ryan in astonishment. Both elves chorused, "A human boy?"

"Sure."

"Aren't you awfully big for a boy?" the stouter one asked. He raised his mushroom to see Ryan better.

"No, I'm about average."

"We heard scientists were coming," the other said.

"Yes, but three of us kids are here with them. *He's* only a child too, you know," Ryan added, nodding toward Punky.

Punky kept on snoring. The elves turned their amazed attention on him, whispering to each other, "A child! That huge creature is only a *child!*" The timid one shuddered. "What must the grown creatures be like!"

"You haven't seen any of us before, then?" Ryan was thinking of the yellow eyes he had seen in the woods at dusk. "Somebody was watching us earlier."

"Probably Hepzibah, just waiting around to cause trouble," the stout elf said disgustedly.

"It's her only talent." The other elf shrugged. "We all have to do what we can."

"Who's Hepzibah?" Ryan asked.

But they seemed to feel they might have said too much already. They shifted uncomfortably, glancing around as though the trouble-making Hepzibah might pounce on them. "Could we change the subject?" the timid one pleaded, his worried eyes quite piteous.

"Sure," Ryan agreed.

The elves waited, small and somehow obedient. Ryan felt rather at a loss. He wondered what Sara, with her good manners, would say if she were in this situation. At last he mustered, "My name is Ryan Finney. Do you have names?"

"Oh yes, yes. I'm Gorth," the stout elf replied eagerly.

"I'm Zender," said the other, with an obliging but clumsy bow. "And if you ever need help, that's *our* talent. Just call us. We live under the sassafras tree, two oaks from the birch grove."

"Why, thank you."

"Yes, you're a kindly human boy. We'd help you." Gorth nodded. "But are the others in your group kind, or cruel? How would they treat us if they got us in their power?"

Ryan thought this over. Would any of the scientists respect the rights of an elf? Or might they regard one as no more than a butterfly, to be slammed into a killing jar? He had no idea.

What about Sara, who had dissected the frog so neatly at school? Of course the frog had been dead already. His sister was tenderhearted, as well as courteous. Still, she might decide to start an elf collection. She had kept an ant farm going for years.

Punky? Who could tell?

"I believe Tracy would be kind," he said finally,

"but I'm not sure about anyone else." He explained who Tracy was, then asked the elves, "How did you hear our expedition was coming to the island?"

"The ghost crew told the mermaids, and the mermaids told us," Zender explained matter-of-factly.

Ryan was staggered by this answer. "Mermaids?"

"Haven't you seen or heard them yet?"

The bell-like voice, the huge flipping fishtail. . . . "Maybe I have."

"You should have pitched your tent farther from the water," Zender said. "Those silly mermaids play around in this cove a lot, especially at night."

"They can be awfully noisy," Gorth agreed.

"I won't mind," Ryan promised, enthralled.

"Well, we hate to rush off," Gorth apologized. "But my toes really are so cold. Where did you say I might find my shoe?"

"Third tent from here, near the woods. Watch out for Dr. Dank, though. And I wouldn't trust Professor Tendril too far, either."

The elves thanked him profusely. Lighting the way with their mushrooms, they opened the tent flap and left.

An instant later the flap was pushed open again. Gorth stuck his head in, and whispered warningly, "Watch out for Hepzibah. I like you, Ryan, so please —watch out for Hepzibah." With that he was gone again, leaving Ryan distinctly uneasy.

Who was this Hepzibah, where was she, and what was she likely to do?

Punky's snoring stopped abruptly. In the dark, his loud voice blared, "I fooled you all, didn't I?"

"Punky! Were you awake right along?"

"Sure I was. My mom's always making me go to bed too early. I pretend to be asleep, and find out lots of interesting things that way."

"Did you see the elves?"

"Sure, I snuck a peek at them." He added indignantly, "If I had them in my power, I'd be kind. I don't know why you didn't trust me."

"I hardly know you," Ryan reminded him. "And I hope you won't tell your parents about them. You talk an awful lot."

"I won't. They wouldn't believe me anyway."

"Dr. Murk certainly was right when he said this island isn't like any place else, wasn't he?"

"It's different from Syracuse," Punky answered readily. "But I haven't traveled much. I don't know about Albany or Rochester."

"Do you suppose Dr. Murk suspects there are elves here? And maybe other fairy-tale people?"

"He might. This trip could be to find out for sure."

"Gorth and Zender said they live in the woods. I wish I'd asked who's behind the stone wall."

"And I wish we knew more about Hepzibah."

Each of the boys lay quiet and wakeful in his sleeping bag. Birds and frogs and insects were quiet now. The island was very still.

But just as Ryan was noticing this, a faint chiming broke the silence. It was a charming sound, as though somewhere a bell had giggled. It was followed by a high, pretty scrap of song, and then another bell-like giggle.

"Listen," Ryan whispered tensely.

"I am." Punky, too, spoke in an awed whisper, instead of shouting as usual.

"Do you suppose it's—could it possibly be—?"

"Let's go down to the beach and see," Punky proposed.

The boys hopped out of their sleeping bags into the chilly dark. Quickly they pulled clothes on over their pajamas.

Outside, the sky was spattered with stars. How huge and white they looked, spread above the ocean thick as daisies in July! In the midst of them, the high thin moon dusted the night with silver. Tips of waves in the cove caught the silver and flashed it back again, a game of light-toss from sky to sea. The spangling, changing bits of brilliance made the whole ocean look alive.

Then, as they reached the sand of the beach, Ryan saw that something *was* alive out there in the water. The chiming giggles could be heard more distinctly now, and one—two—three—four heads bobbed above the surface of the sea, trailing long seaweed hair.

Ryan could make out an assortment of white hands and arms, swimming and splashing playfully. Another head appeared; then two or three dove beneath the surface. Big fishtails, scales gleaming in the moonlight, flailed up instead.

"They're playing, just like the elves said," Punky whispered.

"And they really are mermaids." As he spoke, Ryan felt a surge of joy. It had taken a lot to convince him, beyond doubt, of the ghost ship. With the elves he had still been incredulous, at least for a few seconds.

But the mermaids seemed so absolutely right, so lovely with their weedy hair and chiming voices, romping in the starlight. They seemed to go perfectly with the wet salt smell of the sea, and the lacy foam breaking against the rocks.

Ryan had spent so much of his life near the ocean. Now it was as though something had always been missing. He had seen whales, sharks, squid. He had watched migrating scallops, seals, eels. But how empty the ocean was until you knew, once and for all, that there were mermaids!

He ran ahead of Punky to the very edge of the water, wanting to see them better, propelled by joy. A mermaid caught sight of him, and another, and then another. Their bell voices rang with alarm. Most dove away. Just two remained, poised in the water, not far from the beach. Ryan could see their faces quite well. One was as pretty as a lotus, the other hopelessly plain.

"Oh, Mer Blossom, look. It's a human boy," the pretty one exclaimed, the words pattering like music notes. Ryan recognized her voice. He was sure she was the one he had heard singing the day before.

"I can see what it is, Llura," the other answered

tartly. "I've seen as many boys as you have on passing ships. Actually there are two of them," Mer Blossom added, as Punky joined Ryan at the shore.

"Boys, are you here with the scientists?" Llura asked.

"Yes. Punky's parents are weather experts, and my father studies fish," Ryan said.

There was a commotion in the water. The heads of some of the other mermaids bobbed up again. "Studies fish? How does he do that?" Mer Blossom asked.

"He—well, sometimes he catches them," Ryan said apologetically.

Tails flew up. Again most of the mermaids dove away, leaving only Llura and Mer Blossom. "*Catches* them," Llura gasped. "How disgusting."

Under the circumstances, Ryan felt he could not deny it.

"Would *you* ever catch a fish?" Mer Blossom asked sternly.

"Perhaps never again," he answered, quickly. "Let *me* ask *you* some questions now. Why does this island have so many—uh—beings that don't seem to exist anywhere else? I've read about you, of course—in story-books—"

"We prefer to call them history books," Mer Blossom corrected. "They're all true, you see. Once the sea was full of mermaids. Every country had its share of elves. And many places, especially in northern Europe, had enchanted kingdoms, like the one behind the stone wall."

"An enchanted kingdom!" Ryan exclaimed.

"Cinderella married above herself and ruled one very successfully," Llura recalled. "She was a terrific housekeeper, I believe."

"Sleeping Beauty and Snow White did well too," Mer Blossom commented. "Although each had her share of trouble along the way. Anyhow—"

"Is there really—really and truly—an enchanted kingdom right here on this island?" Punky interrupted to ask eagerly. "Is that honestly what's behind the stone wall?"

"Of course." Mer Blossom spattered a wavelet with one hand. "As I was saying, there used to be magic everywhere in the world, just as the history books record it. But it's been dying out. *We've* almost died out. This island is the last stronghold of an endangered species."

"We're living fossils, really." Llura floated on her back, right on the surface of the water. Her scales glittered like flakes of mica. "I suppose that's why the old scientist brought the others here to study us."

"What's the kingdom like?" Ryan asked, fascinated.

"Well, there's a castle that's supposed to be absolutely spectacular." Mer Blossom swam in circles, chasing her tail, till she grew dizzy.

"Once upon a time a good king lived in the castle," Llura said. Sadness crept into her voice. "But he's dead now. A lot of nasty hobgoblins have taken over the grounds, we've heard."

"They threw stones at the old scientist." Mer Blossom giggled. "Did he tell you?"

"Yes. Who else lives behind the wall?" Punky asked.

"Wizards and witches and fairy godmothers, and all kinds of enchanted people. We only know what we hear. We can't get inside, of course," Mer Blossom pointed out.

"Yet I was meant to be queen of that kingdom." Llura spoke more sadly still. "I would have been as good a housekeeper as Cinderella. As sweet-natured as Sleeping Beauty. As nice to dwarfs as Snow White."

"And as modest as the queen who kept asking, 'Who's the fairest one of all?'" Mer Blossom said with a touch of sarcasm.

"I was meant to live in that castle," Llura rushed on. She sat up in the water, facing the beach, bobbing dolefully on little waves. "I would have eaten strawberries and whipped cream, which are said to be delicious. Nightingales would have sung for me. A thousand servants would have done my bidding."

"How could you live on land?" Ryan asked, puzzled.

"I—"

"Llura, why didn't we think of it before?" Mer Blossom interrupted. "Only a human boy can break the evil spell, remember. And here are two of them!"

"Why—why of course!" Llura exclaimed. "How wonderful—" She swam closer to shore, and called with rising hope, "Oh boys, human boys, have you come to get back the magic jewel? Have you come to save us from the terrible Wizard of the Wind?"

"Not me," Punky answered promptly.

"We have no particular plans," Ryan added with almost equal haste.

In a movement of liquid grace, Llura climbed onto a rock only a few yards from where they were standing. Ryan saw she was slender and short by human standards, somewhere in size between a large carp and a small sturgeon. Her lovely face was full of distress. "Do you know how the Wizard has ruined my life?"

"No, we don't," Ryan admitted.

"Let me tell you, then. One of you may be the hero we've been waiting for."

Chapter

6

LLURA BEGAN by explaining that she was the youngest daughter of the King of the Sea.

"He's very old now, and hasn't really ruled the ocean in ages," Mer Blossom put in. She swam in idle circles, occasionally patting the water to scatter silver droplets of reflected moonshine.

"Still, I'm a princess." Llura tossed her seaweed hair. "I also happen to be the prettiest mermaid still in existence."

"There aren't many of us left," Mer Blossom commented dryly.

"I suppose I was spoiled. Adorable, but spoiled. Just drifting in the shallows, changeable as the tide."

"She was," Mer Blossom affirmed.

"I could have married any merman I wanted. A couple of minor wizards were in love with me too. But *I* never fell in love with anybody."

"Too frivolous," Mer Blossom explained.

"Until one day, as I was sitting on a rock singing and luring sailors to destruction—"

"Hold on a minute there," Ryan interrupted, confused. "You were doing *what?*"

"Llura, let me explain this part. You're making a mess of it." Mer Blossom's plain face was embarrassed. She told the boys earnestly, "We don't really *want* sailors to wreck their ships on these rocks. But sometimes when we're singing, they do come in awfully close to shore, to listen to us. Accidents happen."

Ryan thought of the black-browed captain. "Is that how the pirate ship was lost?"

"Yes. And it's too bad, because the captain had a wife and children at home," Mer Blossom said. "We heard they came to the island to search for the captain, after the wreck. They hoped to find him still alive. They met with some sort of accident themselves, I believe, but I'm not sure what happened. We were sorry. *I* was, anyway." She threw a reproachful glance at Llura, who looked unrepentant.

Ryan remembered the captain's wistful expression when he had watched Sara and Punky feed the gulls. Did he like children, then?

"Now, of course, he must sail these waters forever," Llura said, with what struck Ryan as heartless unconcern.

"Why?" Punky asked.

"It's just how things are," she answered carelessly. "Some wizard or another made the rule, I suppose. Or perhaps a witch decided it, long ago. Anyway, to get back to the main point." Her voice grew tender, and very sorrowful. "I was singing one day when a royal sailing ship drew near. A handsome landling Prince was on it. We fell in love at first sight. He jumped overboard and swam out to my rock. Every day after that he came to visit me."

"His father was the King of the Castle." Mer Blossom scattered moonlight, splish-splash. "The family lived here on the island, behind the stone wall."

"The King was very powerful," Llura said.

Punky whispered to Ryan, "People here keep talking about power."

"They do that everywhere," Ryan told him.

"The King owned a magic jewel and could cast spells with it. But he was good, and was careful not to make anyone unhappy. His spells were always nice ones," Llura said.

"When the Prince told him how much he loved Llura, the King agreed to turn her into a landling," Mer Blossom explained.

"I was to have legs," Llura's sad voice chimed. "And dresses with diamonds on them, prettier than scales. And marry my Prince, and live happily ever after."

Mer Blossom went on with the story. "The King was not the only one who found out that Llura and the Prince were in love. One of the minor wizards, who wanted her for himself, heard she was to marry another. He was furious, and vowed this would never happen."

"He raged around, but we didn't pay any attention. He had so little power then, you see," Llura continued. "He was only a wizard of light breezes, really."

"Couldn't do much more than stir a leaf," Mer Blossom added. "But on the very night before Llura was to be transformed into a landling, the Wizard blew into the castle through a crack in the ceiling. The King was sleeping. So were all the members of the royal court. The Prince was down in the cove, sitting on a rock with Llura."

"So it was easy for the Wizard to steal the magic jewel. As soon as he found it, he used one spell to give himself great power over the winds. Then he blew the jewel out of the castle. When he had it hidden away, he—he—" Llura seemed almost overcome by the horror of what she had to relate. "He used the second spell to turn my beloved Prince into—into—"

"Into a flounder," Mer Blossom said matter-of-factly.

"Oh, it was so terrible," Llura wailed. She began to cry. Tears ran down her lovely face. The other mermaids bobbed up here and there in the water. They, too, were crying. Even Mer Blossom seemed affected by the sadness of it all. She swam in slow circles, not playing anymore.

Llura sobbed, "There we were on the rock, my Prince and I, kissing each other and holding hands. And suddenly he *had* no hands. Only fins. I tossed him into the sea—"

"She had to, you know," Mer Blossom explained. "They can't live out of water."

"I know," Ryan replied, dazed. A flounder. Could such a thing be true? Well, if there could be a mermaid, why not?

"Can this flounder talk, by any chance?" he asked, remembering the story about the fisherman who caught the enchanted fish.

"Of course," Llura answered. "He can offer to grant a wish to escape death."

"Enchanted princes have that right, no matter what they're turned into," Mer Blossom said. "It's a courtesy that's always extended to royalty."

"Wishes don't always turn out quite as one expects, though," one of the other mermaids added.

"No, there's always a certain risk," Mer Blossom agreed.

Ryan was thinking anxiously of what Dr. Murk had said to his father, about catching an unusual fish. How awful it would be if—

"Luckily you get only two spells with a stolen magic jewel," Mer Blossom commented. "Otherwise there's no telling what else the Wizard would do."

"My Prince—just a flat, ugly little flounder. Yet I love him still. It happened long ago," Llura mourned. "The King is dead. They say a dear old fairy godmother still lives in the castle, with a few aging servants. The godmother of our child, she would have been, if we could have married and had one—" she sobbed.

"Because Llura was once so foolish and changeable, the Wizard thought she would soon forget, and marry him instead," Mer Blossom explained.

"But I won't. Never, never, never."

As Llura said this, a strong billow of wind passed over the water. The waves roughened. All in a moment, a storm had begun.

"Oh, Mer Blossom, it's the Wizard," Llura cried. Again the wind blew like a mighty gust of anger, and the waves grew higher.

"He must want to stop us from telling the boys," Mer Blossom shouted above the rising gale. "Oh, boys, listen—there has to be a way of breaking every spell, but the Wizard made it hard, very hard."

Again the wind roared. Llura shrieked against it, "The only way my Prince can become a landling again is for a human boy to steal the magic jewel back, and return it to him."

"The Wizard thought no human boy would ever come here," Mer Blossom yelled above the storm. "It's off the beaten track, you know." A high wave rose behind her and crashed over her. She vanished, then bobbed up again, gurgling, "But you're here, you're here at last—and if you can get the jewel and return it to the Prince, the Wizard's power will leave him—"

The wind blew furiously at this. Suddenly the moon and stars went dark. Trembling, Ryan looked up at the sky. A gigantic black form, with outspread bat-like black wings, was sweeping over the sea.

"The Wizard!" Ryan gasped.

"The Wizard!" Punky echoed.

Ryan grabbed Punky's arm and pulled him back, just as a towering wave crashed before them on the beach. Terrified, both boys turned and ran from the lashing tempest. Pleading voices followed them, wailing, "Boys! Boys! Get back the jewel! The Wizard keeps it in the Cavern of the Winds!"

Ryan half expected to be blown away at any instant, or pursued by a wave and swept out to sea. But to his amazement, he and Punky found themselves running from nothing. The wind died down as quickly as it had risen.

At a little distance from the shore, the boys dared to look back. The water was still ruffled, but the worst waves were subsiding. The mermaids had gone. Stars and the slender moon shone calmly in the sky again.

"I hated that," Punky burst into tears. He rubbed his fists into his eyes. "That's the most scared I've ever been."

"Me too. But it seems to be over now," Ryan told him shakily. "Here come Sara and Tracy. I suppose that gale woke everybody up."

Tracy and Sara ran along the beach toward them. "Are you all right?" Sara called anxiously.

"I've never known a storm to come and go so fast," Tracy said. "It was horrible."

Ryan was surprised to see the tents still standing, undamaged. Then he realized the Wizard had been content just to terrify them. It was a warning, a threat. Having shown them his power, he had blown away, leaving the campsite untouched.

Mr. and Mrs. Gust ran from their tent carrying

weather instruments. "Wasn't that something! Utterly weird!" They sounded more pleased than anything else. "Everybody safe?"

"I think so." Tracy nodded. "Nothing's happened to any of the tents."

Mr. and Mrs. Gust bustled to the shore. They studied their instruments, talking about barometric readings and low pressure centers. Sara followed them. So did the scientists, as they spilled one by one from the tents, dazed with sleep.

Tracy and Ryan and Punky stayed together. It seemed to Ryan that Tracy sensed how scared they had been, and how threatened they still felt. She spoke soothingly about the quiet that had come over the island again. She pointed out how beautiful the stars were. Punky stopped crying, and Ryan began to feel better.

Then she asked, "Are there manatees out there? Sara and I thought we heard voices, when the wind was at its strongest."

Ryan knew the manatee is a sea mammal that can often be heard near the ocean. If anyone else except Punky had been nearby, he would have said yes. Instead, it struck him that this, finally, was an opportunity to tell Tracy about the books in Dr. Murk's cabin, the vanishing ship, Gorth and Zender, the mermaids, the Wizard, everything.

"No, it was—" Punky began loudly.

Ryan gagged him by placing a hand firmly over his mouth. "I'll do the telling. Okay?"

Punky shook off the hand and lifted his chubby chin, as he did when he was offended. But he did not say anything more.

Softly, so as not to be overheard, Ryan began.

As he went on, Tracy's blue eyes grew as wide and full of wonder as a child's. When he got to the part about the flounder, he saw that she shared his apprehensions. And when he told her about the Wizard bringing the storm, she looked frightened.

"You two could have been badly hurt. Please, boys, be careful—" her voice dropped to a whisper. Ryan saw his father and Dr. Murk strolling toward them over the sand.

"And in the morning, I'll show you the drawing of the fish," Dr. Murk was saying.

"Great," Dr. Finney replied enthusiastically. "I'll hang the nets from the dock, first thing tomorrow."

Chapter

7

BACK IN THEIR TENT, Punky fell asleep quickly, exhausted. But Ryan turned and tossed in his sleeping bag, trying to decide what to do. Never before had he felt such a heavy sense of responsibility.

The Prince must be warned, but he could not think how to do this. Even more worrisome, the Prince's fate, and Llura's happiness, seemed to rest squarely on Ryan's shoulders. It was unlikely that Punky would get the magic jewel back, and it might be decades before another human boy came here.

The very thought of angering the Wizard made Ryan break out in a sweat. Besides, he didn't know where the Cavern of the Winds was. Nor could he imagine how he would return the jewel to the Prince even if he had it.

No, it was all impossible. He would never forget his terror when that gigantic bat-like figure had blotted out the sky. He remembered the crashing waves, the howling wind. But he remembered, too, the little mermaid pleading, "Oh boys, human boys. . . ."

What was the good of being human, if you turned away when somebody needed you?

So Ryan kept going back and forth over everything in his mind.

At length he came to the conclusion that he would get up very early in the morning, find a mermaid, and see if she could get a message to the Prince. That was one problem that could not wait. If the flounder came swimming around the dock after his father got those nets out, it would be the end. He could decide later what, if anything, to do about the magic jewel.

With this course of action decided upon, Ryan finally fell into a restless sleep. He was awakened just at dawn by a rustling of the tent flap. He sat up, expecting to see Gorth and Zender. Instead, he found himself looking into a pair of yellow eyes.

It was the black cat. Ryan stared at it, feeling almost hypnotized. There was something evil in its fixed golden gaze.

"Hepzibah?" he asked uncertainly.

The cat hissed and spat, as though disliking the fact that he knew its name.

Now Ryan felt sure this really was the trouble-making Hepzibah that Gorth and Zender had told him about. For a moment he was afraid the cat might spring at him, so vicious did it look. But it turned and slunk out of the tent, with only one piercing backward glance.

Ryan was shaken. He was waking up to enough problems without adding anything more. His responsibilities crowded in on him again.

He was glad, at least, that the cat had awakened

him early. Quickly he found his sneakers. He had left on the rest of his clothes when he went to sleep. There was so much going on in this place that it hardly seemed worthwhile ever getting undressed.

He left the sleeping Punky in the tent, and hurried down to the shore. The first pale dawn light was fingering across the sea. The water was calm and soft looking, like gray silk. A few last stars still lingered in the sky.

There was such calm in this dawn that it seemed the whole world must be sleeping. Certainly there was no sign of the mermaids. It occurred to Ryan that sleeping might be exactly what they were doing. They had been up late, romping and playing last night. And the storm had probably taken it out of them; all that rough water, waves crashing over them.

But where did they sleep? How did you contact a sleeping mermaid?

Rather hopelessly, he picked up a few shells and threw them into the sea. He did this on the off chance that he might rouse mermaids from the bottom of the water. But there was no response, and he had not really expected any.

He cast around for other ideas, growing more disturbed by the moment. The fan of sun was spreading wider over the sea. His father was an early riser, eager about his work. Those nets were likely to be hanging off that dock within an hour or so.

"Mer Blossom!" he called softly. "Llura!" He did

not dare shout for fear of awakening the scientists in their tents.

And still the sea was as tranquil and unbroken as a boundless bolt of fabric.

Ryan rubbed his hand over his hair distractedly. If only he and Tracy had had more time to talk the night before, she might have come up with some plans. He could not speak to her now without waking Sara. But he needed a friend.

He thought of Punky, and considered going back and waking him up. Punky was so loud about everything, though. And he probably tended to blurt out the truth to the wrong people.

His father? Ryan loved him dearly, but he did not want to try explaining to him that he was trying to get a message to a flounder by way of a mermaid. And to keep him out of his father's nets, too.

What other friend did he have? Who might help?

Then he thought of Gorth and Zender. Helping was their talent, they had said. Of course, they were just the ones. They would know where mermaids slept, and how to rouse one, if anybody did.

He ran quietly up the beach and into the woods. It was lovely at this time of the morning, cool and fresh, with dew on the ferns and mosses. Spider webs were scattered like lace on the grasses. Mushrooms, in a variety of shapes and sizes, grew from old fallen logs and from brown leaf mold. Birds sang.

Ryan loved the woods, and could have spent days

looking and listening. But there was no time now.
He hurried on, until he came to the birch grove. He
continued past two large oaks, to a sassafras tree. The
ground beneath it was strewn with mushrooms. He
saw what looked like several chuck holes.

"Gorth?" he called. "Zender?" Not knowing what
else to do, he knocked on the bark of the sassafras tree.
"Is anybody home?"

Here and there, little heads in leafy green caps
peeped out of the holes in the ground. Elf eyes looked
up. But when they saw Ryan, they darted out of sight
again.

"I'm a friend," Ryan assured them. "I won't harm
anybody. And Gorth and Zender said to call them if
I needed help."

"Oh. Help," several of the piping voices said.
"That's different. We like to help." A few came bravely
out of their holes, while others rustled around underground. Ryan heard them saying sharply, "Gorth!
Zender! Wake up! It's a chance to help!"

How nice elves are, Ryan thought gratefully. Not
selfish at all. So ready and willing.

In only a moment, Gorth and Zender tumbled out
of their holes, yawning but smiling. Ryan noticed
Gorth had both shoes on. "I'm so glad you got your
shoe back," he said.

"Thanks to you," Gorth replied. "Now tell us, what
can we do for you?"

Ryan outlined the situation. He was embarrassed

at having to explain that his own father was about to catch the Prince. But the elves were tactful, and did not comment on that part of the story.

"The trouble is, mermaids usually sleep out beyond the reefs," Gorth said. "And they're lazy. They probably won't stir from there until ten or so."

"I'll swim out there and find one for you," Zender offered enthusiastically, his timid face aglow.

"You don't know how to swim, Zender," Gorth reminded him. "None of us do."

Zender looked downcast. "That's right, I keep forgetting."

"I have it!" Gorth snapped his fingers. "The King of the Sea gets up much earlier than the mermaids do. He's usually in one of the coves by now, singing morning songs and greeting the dawn. He's Llura's father, you know. So he'd be sure to find her. He'd do anything to save her Prince."

"Wonderful! Do you have any idea which cove I might find him in?"

"Yes, it's just near here. Come, we'll show you," Gorth offered.

Despite their small size, the elves ran quickly through the woods, with Ryan close behind. They ran through a pumpkin patch—huge, the pumpkins were —and past several towering vines. The vines went up and up into the sky, so high that the tops of them could not be seen. They were covered with bean pods, each nearly as large as an elf.

"Why—these are magic beanstalks," Ryan marveled. "Like the one Jack grew."

"We never knew Jack, although we've heard about him," Gorth said, pausing beside one of the beanstalks.

"Are there giants rumbling around up there, going 'Fee fi fo fum'?" Ryan asked.

"We've never climbed up to find out," Zender told him.

"Sometimes six or eight of us get together and eat a bean," Gorth said. "They're a pleasant change from mushrooms. Try one."

Ryan snapped off a pod, ate part of a bean, and stuffed the rest in his pocket for later. It had a good flavor, and there was no telling how long it would be before he got any breakfast.

"The cove is just ahead." Gorth led them on again.

Even before they reached the beach, Ryan heard a rusty voice, a voice like a cracked old bell, singing a happy song. The words came to him clearly:

"I join the angelfish in prayer,
 And porpoises at play.
 I shake hands with an octopus
 No less than twice a day.

"My subjects always welcome me.
 It's clearly understood
 That though I am their monarch,
 I am jolly, wise, and good.

"I sleep at night on beds of weed.
The starfish light my sky,
And mermaids, wandering through the deep,
Sing me a lullaby.

"I rule this cool salt kingdom
Where it's always best to be,
And I love this lovely morning
In the lovely, lovely sea. . . ."

"There he is," Zender said as they reached the beach.

On a rock in the water near shore sat an ancient merman, with hair and beard of gray seaweed. His scales did not glitter as brightly as the mermaids' had; they were dull with age. As he moved a bit on the rock, it was evident that his fishtail was stiff with arthritis.

He had none of the youthful bounce that the mermaids had. Yet he looked quite cheerful, basking alone in the warming sun. He held a large shell in one hand, and waved it in time to his song.

"Do you need us anymore?" Zender asked Ryan.

"No, you've been great. Thank you." The elves departed, and Ryan called, "Pardon me, Your Majesty."

The King turned to look at him. A beautiful welcoming smile spread over his old face. "You're a human boy! The mermaids told me you were here, but it seemed too good to be true. Oh, human boy, will you try to get the magic jewel back?"

"I—I don't know. But something even more important has to be done right now—" He explained about the nets.

The old King listened gravely. He understood the danger, and acted promptly. "I'll call the mermaids with my shell. It's loud enough to be heard even beyond the reefs."

He puffed up his cheeks and blew mightily into the shell. Sure enough, it made a tremendous blast. He blew into it again, and again. Two dolphins appeared, and a small whale, and then a sleepy-looking mermaid.

Soon mermaids were thronging into the cove, perhaps a dozen of them, chiming in agitation: "What is it, oh King? What's the matter?"

Ryan saw Llura among them. Again he told the bad news, asking, "Can you find the flounder? Will you be able to warn him?"

"Yes, yes, I will—I must," Llura replied frantically. "He usually swims right around the island. He wants to stay near me, you know."

"We'll look too," the other mermaids chimed. The dolphins clicked in agreement, and Ryan thought he saw a nod from the whale.

"If you could get him to stay out beyond the reef, it would be best," Ryan said. "My father starts the nets off the dock. Then, if he has no luck, he usually goes out in a boat. But not very far out, at first, especially for flounders. So often they're in near shore."

"Oh, dreadful, dreadful," the mermaids murmured. They dove away. Ryan could see them all swimming strongly beneath the surface: mermaids, dolphins, whale. The King waved to Ryan and followed the others more slowly, his arthritic tail moving stiffly in the water.

So the desperate search began. Ryan felt relieved that his part of it was over. He turned to walk back through the woods—and found himself face to face with Dr. Murk, who stepped out from behind a tree.

Chapter

8

"I WONDERED if one of you children would be the first to discover the secret," the old scientist said.

"I—I didn't know you were there," Ryan stammered. "What—what brought you to this cove?"

"The old King's shell trumpet. That was quite a blast."

Ryan did not know what to say. Dr. Murk must have heard most of his conversation with the mer-people.

"Even I never dreamed my discoveries would be so glorious. I can see it now." The old scientist looked inspired. "A display of creatures we will bring back from this expedition."

"What do you mean?" Ryan asked with dread.

"The flounder, of course. He is bound to be caught. And in the same tank with him, a mermaid or two. I will have an imitation rock made, of concrete perhaps."

The thought made Ryan feel sick. He remembered Llura and Mer Blossom playing in the moonlight, and pictured them cooped up in a tank with people gaping at them.

Dr. Murk went on, "And nearby, a cage of elves,

under a plastic tree. Styrofoam mushrooms, of course. . . ."

Friendly Gorth and Zender, taken from their moist leafy woods, not able to help anyone ever again.

"You couldn't do such an awful thing," Ryan cried passionately.

"But it's just what I will do. I will be one of the most famous scientists who ever lived." Dr. Murk's look of inspiration hardened into one of cold ambition. "My wish has come true, as the flounder promised."

"What? What are you talking about?"

"Some years ago, I was fishing in these waters. I caught the flounder. It astonished me by saying, 'Fisherman, fisherman, pray let me go, and I will grant any wish you may desire.' I wished to make one more important scientific discovery before I died. The flounder said, 'Your wish will be granted,' and I threw him back into the sea."

Again Ryan saw the glint of ambition in the scientist's eyes. He remembered how faraway and gentle the old man had seemed on the journey here, and felt stunned and bewildered by the change in him.

"I had rented a little boat just for the day," Dr. Murk went on. "When I returned to the inn where I was staying, I found boxes and boxes of books in my room. They were all fairy tales. I realized that somehow, by some magic, the fish was trying to tell me something."

He described how he had spent years studying and reading the books, slowly coming to the conclusion that somewhere these fairy-tale creatures still lived. "After all, I already knew about the talking fish. So it was not too hard to believe in the others. And I decided the place was probably not far from where I had caught him."

On the mainland, he had heard rumors of a ghost ship. It sounded like an ideal vessel in which to search for an enchanted kingdom.

"I think you know the rest," Dr. Murk told Ryan. "I rented the ship and crew, and we kept sailing these waters. I explored one little island after another. Then I found the elf bones, and knew I had come to the right place."

"Dr. Murk, please. You *have* made the important discovery. Your wish has been granted. But these creatures have lives of their own to live, just as we do. Please, please—" Ryan could hardly find words for what he felt. His eyes blurred with tears and his throat closed up.

He saw that Dr. Murk was not even listening. He turned and walked away through the woods. Ryan followed silently, raging in his heart.

At the campsite, Dr. Dank was complaining that the mushrooms and shoe he had found the night before had disappeared. Tracy was flipping pancakes in a big pan over the fire. She did it expertly, sending each cake sailing into the air. Professor Finney watched her, laughing.

Ryan looked beyond them to the dock. He saw the nets hanging from it into the water.

"Oh, Finney," Dr. Murk said casually, "I have reason to believe you'll get that fish quicker if you go out beyond the reefs."

"Oh? I'll take a boat and do that, then, right after breakfast," Professor Finney agreed.

Despair seized Ryan. Had he gone through all this, only to send the flounder into his father's nets? The mer-people would probably think he had done it on purpose.

He looked at Dr. Murk with real hatred. The old scientist's eyes glinted craftily.

At that moment, Ryan decided, in his deep anger and sense of outrage, to try to steal the magic jewel from the Wizard. How or when he would be able to do it, he did not know. But he would try.

Yet again the first problem was to keep the flounder safe. He made a hasty decision, the only one he could think of. "Dad," he asked his father, "can I take one of the boats and a net? I'd like to go out for a while now."

"No breakfast first?" Tracy asked.

"No," he said firmly. She did not urge him, and he thought she realized something important was happening.

She murmured only, "Be careful."

"Sure, go ahead," Professor Finney said. He was always pleased by Ryan's love of the sea. "Why don't you go along too, Sara, and work on your seaweed collection?"

Ryan's heart sank. He hoped Sara would turn down

75

the idea. But she finished a pancake she was eating, and joined Ryan readily.

Well, with or without her, he had to get out beyond those reefs before his father did—had to give the mermaids another message, or catch the flounder himself and warn him, or do *something*.

If his father did catch the fish, and it offered to grant him a wish, he wondered if his father would let it go free. He doubted it. He could not imagine his father taking a bribe of any kind. He was a man who did his job as well as he could, and expected no special favors.

"I'll row us out. You can row us back," Sara said as they got into one of the boats. She tied a net over the side, to pick up seaweed.

Ryan had a net, too, between his feet on the bottom of the boat. He decided that when they got beyond the reefs, he would try calling the fish first. With luck, it might surface. He could explain the situation to it then, and not have to net it at all.

What should he call it? Prince? It sounded somehow like calling a dog. Yet to call someone Flounder seemed rude.

His hands grew clammy with nervousness. What was Sara going to think when he started doing this calling? Maybe he should try to prepare her now. But he knew what her reaction would be. It was useless.

This was going to be embarrassing, no question about it.

The ideal thing, of course, would be to run into

a mermaid. With proof right before her eyes, Sara could be convinced. But in the calm flat sea, there was not one to be seen.

He thought of how the water had looked last night during the storm, and a knot of dread tied up his stomach. Where was the Wizard now? Hopefully he was a late riser, still asleep in his cavern. Not a breath of air seemed to be stirring. But what if he woke up?

Sara was rowing steadily. Ryan looked behind him. They were pretty far out from the beach. If the Wizard blew up a storm now, they would be trapped in gale winds and crashing waves.

"Row faster," he said to Sara. "Let's get this over with."

She looked at him indignantly. "If you don't like how I'm doing, you can take over the oars yourself."

"No, it's okay, I'm sorry." She rowed better than he did, and they both knew it.

The reefs were still some distance ahead. In Ryan's adventurous life, he had learned that panic is the worst enemy. When there was nothing you could do about what worried you, it was best to try to think of something else, preferably something pleasant.

The image of Tracy flipping pancakes came into his mind.

"What are you brooding about, anyway?" Sara asked. "You're acting funny this morning."

Ryan hesitated. He did not like to mention Tracy directly, but he did say, "I wish we had a stepmother."

There was a sudden thrashing sound from the net

in the water. A mellow male voice called up from it, "Fisherman, fisherman, pray set me free, and I will grant your wish."

Sara's mouth fell open. She nearly dropped the oars. Ryan reached over the side and pulled up the net. A large flounder was caught in it. It looked at Ryan with intelligent pleading eyes.

Ryan was buoyant with relief. "I'm going to toss you right back," he assured it happily. "I just came out here to warn you. My father's going to be out beyond the reefs in a little while, trying to catch you. He means well. It's his job, that's all. Anyway, I guess your best bet would be to go around to the other side of the island. Stay away from the dock too."

"Your wish will be granted," the flounder said warmly, with a hint of a smile around the gills.

Ryan disentangled it from the net and dropped it overboard.

"It talked. The fish talked." Sara was holding the oars limply, pale with shock. "The flounder talked to you, Ryan, and you talked to it. And I must be dreaming this."

"No. Here, I'll row us in." He took the oars from her and they changed places. As he rowed back to the beach, he told her everything. Now she believed him. Like Tracy, she looked very frightened when he described the Wizard, and explained about the magic jewel.

"Oh, Ryan, you're not going to try to get the jewel, are you? You might be killed."

"Let's not talk about it out here," he muttered, scanning the sky.

She saw his point. They did not talk anymore until they had tied the boat up and were safely on the dock. Then she said, "Whatever you decide, Ryan, I want you to know I'll help you if I can. I promise."

She was a girl to be trusted. She never broke a promise. It was one of those rare moments when they were aware, brother and sister, of loving each other.

Awkwardly, Ryan said, "Thanks." He noticed that the nets were still hanging from the dock. He was surprised. He had expected his father to be starting out in a boat by this time.

"Look," Sara said in a low astonished whisper.

Ryan saw their father sitting on the beach with a woman he had never seen before. The woman had long black hair. She was wearing a long dress of black velvet and black furry boots. Her face was beautiful. As Ryan and Sara stared at her, she turned to look at them with yellow cat-like eyes, eyes that seemed to gleam with an evil light.

Ryan knew those eyes. His skin crawled.

"Hi, kids." His father waved. "Welcome this stranger who's come to our island. Her boat was wrecked up the beach in the night. I met her here just a few minutes ago, but already it seems—" he gazed at the woman sentimentally, "it seems as though I'd been under her spell a long, long time."

Ryan and Sara were too amazed to reply. There was a small wrecked rowboat up the beach, but Ryan

was sure it had not been there when he had come looking for mermaids earlier this morning. And why would
anybody go out in a boat in that outfit? Where had she
come from? None of it made sense.

"You haven't even told me your name yet," his
father said to the mysterious stranger.

She smiled a curling cat-like smile. "My name is
Hepzibah."

Chapter

9

THE DAY DEVELOPED into the strangest of Sara's and Ryan's life. Their father introduced Hepzibah to the other members of the expedition. He repeated her story of the wrecked boat. Everybody was as puzzled as Sara and Ryan were. Only their father seemed to believe her blindly, without thinking.

"I didn't know there were other islands so near," Mrs. Gust said. "You can't have come very far in these waters, in only a rowboat."

Hepzibah did not answer. She only smiled her curved feline smile.

"Were you going to an—uh—evening party?" Professor Tendril asked. He waved his thin hands in the air to indicate her long dress.

Hepzibah smiled. Professor Finney gazed at her like a love-smitten schoolboy.

Tracy asked no questions. Her hurt showed, at least to Ryan. She sat cross-legged on the ground near the dead campfire, silent and alone. Only half an hour before, she had been flipping pancakes and laughing with their father. Now he seemed to have forgotten she had ever existed.

One by one, the scientists dispersed to pursue their special interests on the island. Tracy wandered away forlornly, with her notebook and camera. Punky looked for shells on the beach. Only Professor Finney lolled on the sand, doing nothing, gazing at Hepzibah.

In her black boots and long dress, she picked her way over to the remains of the campfire. Big frying pans and coffeepots were still there, and some long toasting forks.

"You," Hepzibah said in a commanding tone, to Sara and Ryan, "What are your names?"

They told her, in subdued voices.

"Clean up these pots and pans and forks. They're so smoky and dirty," Hepzibah complained, wrinkling her nose. "I want them to shine, do you understand? To *shine*."

"But—" Sara ventured, "they just get like that from cooking over the fire."

Hepzibah clapped her hands together so sharply both children jumped. Her face clouded with anger. "Don't argue with me. Don't you *dare* argue with me. Just do as I say."

The children turned in bewilderment to their father.

"Don't argue with the lady," he said amiably. "Just do what she says."

Fuming, Ryan and Sara picked up the pots and pans and forks. They found a sponge, and went up the beach to scrub at the smoke stains with sand.

"What's the *matter* with him?" Sara muttered. "He acts as if he's been hypnotized."

"It must be something like that. A spell," Ryan muttered back.

"What right does she have to tell us what to do? She's treating us as if we were—"

An awful thought struck Ryan. He stopped scrubbing, and grabbed his sister's arm. "Sara, do you remember what I said just before we realized the fish was in the net?"

She frowned, trying to remember. "Why, I think you said—you wished we had a stepmother."

"Yes. And he said twice that my wish would be granted."

The two children stared at each other in dawning horror. "You mean Dad may *marry* Hepzibah?"

"She seems to have all the qualifications for a cruel stepmother," Ryan pointed out. "In storybooks, there's no other kind."

"But we've got to stop him," Sara cried.

"I don't know what anybody can do about stopping these spells, once they're underway."

"At least time is on our side," Sara said thoughtfully. "They can't get married here on the island. There's nobody to marry them."

"That's true."

Hepzibah's voice, cruel and sharp, called, "Why are you two taking so long? Those pots should be clean by now. And next I want you to wash down the outsides of the tents. They look dusty. And gather some firewood. And when you've finished with that—"

It went on all day. Sara and Ryan were driven to do one nasty useless job after another. And through it all, their father, who was usually a just man, insisted they follow Hepzibah's ridiculous orders.

"Now I know how Cinderella felt," Sara muttered to Ryan.

"Well, at least she ended up all right." Ryan tried to be comforting.

"I don't know. I'd rather marry a lab technician." Sara sighed, struggling with a huge armload of firewood.

Dr. Dank found some more mushrooms; Professor Tendril found a giant beanstalk; the Gusts waited eagerly for another storm. And still Professor Finney left his nets hanging from the dock, and paid attention only to Hepzibah.

Even Punky realized the oddness of it. He asked Ryan, "What's wrong with your Dad?"

Ryan told him his suspicions, and that the woman in black was the dreaded Hepzibah.

"The one the elves said—?"

"That's right. The troublemaker. And she's off to a good start."

Late in the afternoon, Dr. Murk returned to the campsite from a walk. He saw the nets, still off the dock. Irritated, he snapped at Professor Finney, "You were supposed to go out beyond the reefs after that flounder. Why haven't you?"

Professor Finney shrugged dreamily. He smiled at Hepzibah, who was making out a list of further tasks for Sara and Ryan to do.

"I wanted that fish caught *today*," Professor Murk burst out in a temper. As professor Finney seemed not even to hear, Dr. Murk's face hardened into a mask of ambition and resolve. Angrily he vowed, "I'll catch it myself. If I have to go round and round this island half the night, I'll catch it."

He stalked off, his white dandelion hair drifting around his head. Within minutes, he had piled the nets into a boat and was rowing out to sea.

Punky and Ryan and Sara looked at each other, helpless and distraught. Before they could exchange a word, Hepzibah had ordered the brother and sister off on another round of chores.

The afternoon waned. The setting sun turned the sky pink and gold above the ocean. The water mirrored it, glazed with sunset colors. Long shadows of evening stretched across the sand of the beach, and darkened the wood.

Ryan and Sara, commanded by Hepzibah to build the campfire for the evening meal, heard a rowboat scraping in at low tide. "I've caught it!" Dr. Murk's voice shouted in triumph. "Finney, get a tank ready! I've caught the flounder!" He staggered out of the boat, carrying a bucket.

Hepzibah and Professor Finney were holding hands, sitting under a pine tree at the edge of the woods. They did not stir.

"The least we can do is get that poor Prince out of the bucket and into a tank." Sara, tenderhearted, looked at Ryan with tear-filled eyes.

He nodded, feeling as miserable as she did. His efforts had failed. The worst had come to pass. His reward for everything he had tried to do was a captured Prince, and life with Hepzibah.

He and Sara ran to their father's tent and got a tank. They filled it with sea water near the dock. Ryan wondered if he could possibly get hold of the bucket and dump the fish into the sea. But Dr. Murk was too clever for that. He held the handle with both hands, watching the children craftily.

From the depths of the bucket, a familiar mellow voice kept repeating, "Fisherman, fisherman. . . ."

"Not this time," Dr. Murk told the fish strongly. "You're going to be Exhibit A—proof that I am a great scientist. Proof of my discoveries."

"Fisherman, fisherman. . . ."

Sara and Ryan could scarcely bear to listen, it was so pitiful. Ryan imagined how Llura would feel when she found out.

Dr. Murk plopped the flounder in the tank. At last the Prince seemed to realize he was beaten. He spoke no more, but lay on the bottom dejectedly. Dr. Murk bore the tank proudly to his tent.

As Ryan watched him go, his own resolve strengthened. He was not going to let this man's ambition separate the mermaid and her Prince forever. He was going to brave the Wizard's fury and steal back the magic jewel. It was the only solution.

"Maybe we can get the Prince out of there while Dr. Murk is sleeping, or something," Sara whispered.

"He'd probably catch him again." Ryan was thinking quickly. He realized there was one advantage to having the flounder in the tank. If he did succeed in finding the jewel, at least he would know where the Prince was, to return it to him.

He told Sara what he had decided. She looked very worried, but said only, "Remember what I promised. Let me help."

He nodded.

"I'm hungry." Hepzibah called imperiously. "Haven't you children got that fire ready yet? Hurry up!"

Sara and Ryan dragged off to do her bidding. Soon the fire was crackling brightly. Dr. Murk brought out some hot dogs and canned potato salad. Everyone gathered, sitting in the circle of the fire's glow, just as they had the evening before.

But how different everything was now! Last night at this hour, Ryan had not met Gorth and Zender yet, nor the mermaids. He had not known the Prince's story. And Tracy and his father had been sitting together, talking, looking so happy.

Now Tracy sat a little apart from everyone, her red head bent, eyes on the ground. She did not seem to care about eating. Professor Finney sat with Hepzibah. In the firelight, her eyes looked to Ryan like golden globes of evil.

"Dr. Murk, I have a favor to ask you," Professor Finney said. He took Hepzibah's hand. "This sweet lady and I have decided to marry. Will you get in touch with the ship's captain by radio, and ask him to return here? He can marry us. The sooner the better."

"Isn't this a little sudden?" Dr. Murk raised his eyebrows.

"Some of the best things in life are sudden," Professor Finney smiled. "A tadpole turns into a frog, and suddenly hops."

The others thought this over. "A mushroom pops up overnight," Dr. Dank contributed. "Full grown."

"Many flowers open in a single day." Professor Tendril nodded.

"Winds change in moments," Mrs. Gust added.

During this conversation, Ryan's feelings boiled like a kettle. He knew Sara felt as he did. Tracy, her chin quivering, looked as though she had been slapped. And Hepzibah had the ugly, glossy air of a winner, with her beautiful face and nasty cat smile.

"All right, I'll radio the captain." Professor Murk went off to his tent. He returned in a minute to report, "The ship will arrive here around nine tomorrow morning."

Ryan groaned. By nine-thirty, he and Sara would have one of the meanest stepmothers in all creation.

Unless—unless—

Suppose he got hold of the magic jewel before that

and gave it to the flounder. Might not the grateful Prince do something to stop the wedding, if Ryan begged him to?

He whispered to Sara, "Let's meet by the shore tonight, when everybody else is asleep. Bring Tracy too."

"What are you going to do?"

"Find out from the mermaids where the Cavern of the Winds is. Then we can plan what to do next."

Chapter
10

THEY GATHERED on the shore when the moon was high, and the sky a daisy field of stars. Punky had stayed awake, so Ryan brought him too. The scientists were asleep in their tents.

They had to wait until nearly dawn before the mermaids came. Then they thronged in. Soon the cove was full of weeping mermaids. The whole sea seemed to flow with their tears. They swam and wept; they sobbed and dove; they cried and floated.

Mer Blossom sat on a rock, her plain face long with grief.

On a nearby rock sat graceful Llura, the saddest of them all, slumped in sorrow.

The King of the Sea swam in stiff arthritic circles around the rock where his daughter mourned.

"So you know about it," Ryan said. "I'm *so* sorry."

He and Punky and Tracy and Sara sat close to each other at the tide line, breathing in the weedy salt-sea smell. They felt bound together by their humanness; and, with the grief of the mer-people before them, they were ashamed.

"Yes, a dolphin told us." Mer Blossom gave a choked sob. "Oh, boy who warned us this morning, was there nothing more you could do to stop it?"

"No." Ryan drew a long breath. "But I *am* going to try to do what you asked me. I want to get the magic jewel from the Wizard, and save the Prince."

"Oh . . . he'll try, he'll try," the mermaids murmured in notes of rising hope.

"We're all terribly sorry," Sara said.

"Yes." Tracy added, "Please don't mistrust me because I'm grown up. I'm on your side."

"Me too," Punky said.

Llura, so forlorn a minute before, smiled radiantly. "Oh, how wonderful it would be—how wonderful—"

"Let's not talk too loud," Ryan put in hastily. He glanced up at the sky. "Does anybody know where the Wizard is now?"

"He's puffing around over the ocean, a few miles out," Mer Blossom answered. "He heard about the Prince being captured."

"And he was glad, the beast," Llura said bitterly. "I told him again how I hate him."

"He may stay away, at least till morning," the King of the Sea guessed. "He seemed to realize it wasn't tactful of him to hang around here, while we're so upset."

"Good." Ryan was relieved, but remained watchful. If the breeze should blow harder, or the water roughen the least bit, he planned to run for his life. "You said

91

he kept the magic jewel in the Cavern of the Winds. Where is that?"

Regretfully, Llura replied, "We don't know, exactly. Except that it's inside the enchanted kingdom, behind the stone wall."

"But how would I find it?"

"The elves might be able to tell you," Mer Blossom suggested. "They go into the kingdom a lot, through underground tunnels."

"All right, I'll ask them. Does the Wizard sleep in the cavern, usually?"

"Oh, no. He's restless, always blowing here and there," Mer Blossom said. "I've heard he just goes in to look at the jewel every once in a while."

"To gloat." Llura was bitter again.

"The big danger is not that he'll catch you while you're actually in the cavern," the King of the Sea said, "but that he'll get you while you're coming or going."

"Oh. Well, thank you." Ryan and his companions stood up.

"Before we go," Tracy said, "can you mermaids tell us anything about a woman named Hepzibah?"

"Hepzibah! How do you know her? I thought she was still being a black cat," Mer Blossom exclaimed.

"She's a woman, at the moment," Tracy replied. "A very nasty one. And she's about to marry a man I—I—I—" her voice broke.

"A man you love?" Llura asked gently.

Tracy nodded. She wiped a tear from her cheek.

"Who is he?" Llura asked, still gentle.

Tracy touched Ryan's shoulder. "This boy's father."

Llura recoiled on her rock. "*His father!* How can you love somebody who catches fish?"

Tracy straightened her shoulders and retorted with spirit, "How can *you* love somebody who *is* one?"

"Let's not quarrel," Sara put in hastily.

"So Hepzibah's going to be a cruel stepmother again," the King of the Sea mused. "Well, I'm not surprised. Every half century or so, she manages to do it."

"She can't keep a marriage going for long," Mer Blossom confided. "A few years at most. *So* ill-tempered. But she does enjoy being a stepmother, and making children miserable."

"I don't see why the Prince wished her on us then," Ryan said indignantly. He explained the circumstances.

"Oh, he can't arrange the details of granting wishes," Llura defended her love. "That's done by someone higher up."

"Who?" Punky asked.

"Probably a Wish Wizard. I'm not sure. Anyway, to answer *your* question," she said to Tracy, "Hepzibah is a black cat when she isn't a woman. She was the mascot on the pirate ship."

"The day the ship was wrecked, she had stayed prowling around on shore," Mer Blossom added. "She missed the journey. That brings bad luck to a ship, you know."

"Hepzibah seems to be bad luck all the way around," Ryan sighed. "And if I don't get the jewel to the

Prince by nine o'clock this morning, she's ours. I'll go speak to the elves right now."

"Go, go, human boy," the mermaids chorused. "Go, and be safe. Get the magic jewel! Get the magic jewel!"

Ryan ran up the beach to the woods, followed by Tracy and Sara and Punky. It was dark among the trees. The white bark on the birches led him to the birch grove. From there it was not hard to find the two oaks. Then a scattering of glowing mushrooms showed up the holes beneath the sassafras tree.

"This is where they live." He knocked on the sassafras bark. "Gorth? Zender? It's an emergency. Wake up."

Soon elves were tumbling sleepily out of the holes, Zender and Gorth among them. Ryan filled them in briefly on what had happened and what he planned to do. "But how can I get inside the wall of the kingdom? What about those hobgoblins? And just where is the cavern, once I get in there?"

"We can help with the hobgoblins," Gorth offered promptly. "We get along with them pretty well. A group of us could go into the kingdom ahead of you, through our tunnels, and attract their attention."

"Invite them to play a game," Zender suggested. "They love games. So do I." His timid face lighted up.

"We'll persuade them to come with us to the playing field," Gorth planned.

"That's beyond the castle grounds, not so near the wall," Zender said.

"It's important that they not see you come into the kingdom. They don't like humans," Gorth warned.

"What would they do if they saw us?" Sara asked.

"Try to stone you to death," Zender replied simply.

"It's too bad you're so enormous," Gorth said. "The only way to get in is through our tunnels. You'd never fit."

Tracy asked, "Isn't there a gate somewhere? The royal family used to go in and out. The Prince was always visiting Llura, we know that."

"The gate is locked and guarded by vicious dragons," Gorth told her. "They *never* sleep."

"They don't like to play, either," Zender said.

"We'll just have to climb up the stone wall somehow," Sara said.

"It's very high, and quite smooth. You couldn't climb it," Zender told her.

"How do the hobgoblins manage to throw stones over it?" Sara asked.

"There are brambles and vines on the inside. They can climb up easily enough, and hurl stones from the top. But the outside is bare," Gorth said.

That gave Ryan an idea. "Okay, come on, let's go," he said eagerly. "Some of you elves can keep the hobgoblins playing, and Gorth and Zender can lead the way to the cavern."

"*Now?*" Gorth exclaimed.

"Sure."

"Ryan." Gorth shook his leafy cap. "Never wake up a hobgoblin."

"No, no." Zender rolled his eyes. "*Never* wake up a hobgoblin. That brings out the worst in them."

"Is there any chance they'd just stay asleep, and we could creep past them?" Ryan asked; but he felt he already knew the answer.

Gorth gave it. "Not a chance. They're very light sleepers."

"When will they get up?"

"With the sun. Not too long to wait," Zender said; and it was true that the wood was less dark than it had been.

"I still don't see how anybody's going to get over the wall," Tracy said.

"I think I've figured that out," Ryan said. "Let's decide about the rest of it."

Some practical matters were discussed. The elves were divided on whether to propose a game of tag to the hobgoblins, or Still Pond No More Moving. When no agreement was reached, Blindman's Buff was decided upon.

The elves judged Tracy too impossibly huge to escape notice in the kingdom. She agreed to return to the campsite and make up an excuse explaining the children's absence to their parents. She would stand ready for that crucial moment when Ryan brought the jewel back, and had to get it into the tank in Dr. Murk's tent.

Sara and Punky would go with Ryan. So would Zender, to show him the entrance to the cavern. "It's small, but I think you can fit in there all right, Ryan."

"Good." The first rays of sun knifed through the trees. "Let's get started."

Led by Gorth and Zender, a small army of elves set off into the deepest part of the forest. The children stayed close behind them.

The trees were taller in here, the mosses greener. Leaf mold covered most of the ground. Little white stems of Indian pipe pushed up through it. The air was cool, close, unmoving.

So the Wizard was not around, not yet, Ryan thought. He took courage from that.

Gorth turned and signaled. All the elves stopped and waited. So did the children. Zender came and whispered, "The stone wall is just ahead. Gorth and the others are going down into the tunnels now, and on into the kingdom." He pointed to a thick pine tree. "Hide behind that pine, so the hobgoblins can't see you. I'll stay with you. When Gorth calls out, 'Say, this is fun!' we'll know he's gotten all the hobgoblins into the game, and it's safe to go over the wall."

Sara and Ryan and Punky nodded, and moved behind the pine. Through its needles, they could make out the stone wall ahead. It went up and up, with no foothold anywhere.

Sara whispered doubtfully to Ryan. "Are you sure you figured out a way for us to get into the kingdom?"

"I'm almost sure," he whispered back.

"Sssh," Zender cautioned.

One by one, the other elves disappeared into holes in the ground. Soon their piping voices could be heard as they emerged into the kingdom. They were answered by hoarse croaks.

"The hobgoblins," Zender told the children softly.

The piping and croaking went on for a few mintues. Ryan caught an occasional word; Gorth and the others were inviting the hobgoblins to play. Then the voices grew more distant. This meant they were moving off to the playing field.

"Say!" Gorth shrilled like a piccolo. "This is fun!"

That was it, the signal that the coast was clear. Ryan and the others ran forward. When they reached the base of the wall, Ryan pulled from his pocket one of the beans he had saved from the giant beanstalk. He pushed it into the ground, right by the wall.

At once, a green shoot appeared from it. The little stalk began to grow. As Ryan watched, it grew and grew, and became a strong vine twining up toward the sky.

Ryan grasped a pair of its leaves and began to climb. He was followed nimbly by Sara and Punky and Zender. Hand over hand they went, higher and higher, until they were level with the top of the wall. Then they jumped onto it, and looked down into the enchanted kingdom.

Chapter
11

RYAN AND PUNKY AND SARA sat on the wall, gazing down, entranced. Zender waited patiently, eating a mushroom; he had seen all of this before.

But how beautiful it was! The most beautiful pictures in Ryan's very best books could hardly compare with it.

Directly below was an overgrown garden, surrounding a fairy-tale castle. The castle was white marble, and seemed to have a thousand windows and towers and balconies.

The garden, wild though it was, charmed Ryan. Red briar roses bloomed against the inner side of the wall, mixed with thick vines. Brilliant goldfish swam in a fish pool. Pumpkins grew here and there. There were lots of weeds—silver bells and cockleshells, they looked like, mostly. And some had pansy faces, like pretty maids in untidy rows.

Ryan liked casual gardens, and here the weeds were almost the best part.

Beyond the castle grounds was a playing field. A lively game of Blindman's Buff was in progress. Gorth wore a blindfold and stumbled around, arms outstretched. Elves and hobgoblins hopped around him.

Ryan saw with interest that the hobgoblins were slightly taller and huskier than the elves. They moved with a peculiar rocking motion, from side to side, croaking and laughing hoarsely. He could not see their faces very well.

A main road wound away from the playing field, a yellow-brick road. Beside it was a luscious gingerbread house, the roof and windows outlined with white frosting and trimmed with gumdrops. Three gingerbread children and a gingerbread woman stood in front of it, holding hands.

Punky pointed excitedly to this group and started to make some loud remark. Sara clapped a hand over his mouth. She whispered, "We'd better keep moving. Somebody might see us up here."

Ryan nodded, and found a foothold in one of the vines. The three children and Zender climbed down quickly. They were scratched by the briars from the roses, but not too badly.

As they reached ground in the garden, the children looked at each other, smiling. They could hardly believe they were actually inside the enchanted kingdom, with Zender, a real elf, beside them.

"Why, it's a girl, isn't it? A darling human girl?" asked a thin sweet voice.

The children turned, startled. Walking toward them along an overgrown path was an old lady, smaller than they were, and oddly dressed. Her dress was of some gauzy material, tattered around the edges. She had wings, also a bit tattered; they were gray, and reminded Ryan of a dusty moth. Her hair fell around her shoulders in long gray curls, and she was carrying a star-tipped wand.

"Yes, I'm a girl," Sara answered. "My name is Sara Finney."

"Who are *you?*" Punky asked.

"I'm a fairy godmother," the old lady said. "And oh, it's been so long since a little girl has come along! I'd love to be *your* fairy godmother, dear." She beamed at Sara.

"That's awfully nice," Sara said politely.

"Let's see, how shall I begin," the fairy godmother murmured. "Oh, I remember." She touched Sara with her wand.

In a twinkling, Sara's jeans and shirt became a fluffy white ball gown. Her sneakers turned into high-heeled glass slippers. Her hair was still in pigtails, which looked strange, but the fairy godmother gazed at her proudly. "I haven't lost the touch, have I?"

"It's—it's pretty." Sara sounded troubled. "But how can I move around in this fancy outfit? It'll get snagged on brambles. And the shoes are *so* uncomfortable. If we have to run, I'm afraid I'll twist an ankle."

Ryan realized she was right. They faced unknown dangers in this kingdom. It was not safe for his sister to be bogged down in clothes like that.

Sara asked, "Fairy godmother, do you know the tragic story of the Prince and the Mermaid?"

"Of course I do, dear. A terrible thing. I had so looked forward to meeting Llura. And the Prince was a great favorite of mine. I've always lived in the castle, you know. And he was the dearest child. I'll never forget—"

"Then you'll be pleased to hear that my brother is going to try to get the magic jewel and break the spell."

"Me too," Punky put in.

The fairy godmother was delighted by this news, and offered to help in any way she could.

"I've got an idea," Zender said suddenly. "I've been worried about getting these large people to the cavern without hobgoblins seeing them. Or dragons."

"Or witches." The fairy godmother nodded.

"Or, worst of all, the Wizard of the Wind," Zender went on. "Why don't you make a pumpkin coach, fairy godmother? The kind without windows, so no one can see in. Turn Ryan into a coachman. I'll sit up front to direct him. Sara and Punky can be hidden inside. We could reach the cavern fast, and get away fast—"

"That's a great idea," Ryan said eagerly.

"So you remember my pumpkin coaches." The fairy godmother beamed at Zender. "Once upon a time, we had coach races every Saturday, on the playing field," she told the children. "Elves against hobgoblins. The whole kingdom would come to watch. But so many of the grand old customs have died out. A shame. Saturdays are boring without—"

"Will you make us a coach now?" Ryan urged her. "Please? Right away?"

"And get me into my regular clothes?" Sara pleaded.

The fairy godmother looked rattled. "Well, let's see. It's so long since I've done a coach, I'm not quite certain—and changing *out* of a ball gown, did I ever do that?" She stood lost in thought, her sweet old face wrinkled with the effort of trying to remember.

Arguing voices came from the playing field. The piping elves and croaking hobgoblins were having a dispute. The hobgoblins accused Gorth of peeking under the blindfold. Some threatened to quit playing unless he was thrown out of the game.

Hearing this, Ryan said in alarm, "Fairy godmother, there's no time to lose. If the hobgoblins stop playing and overrun this garden again, we'll be in mortal danger."

"Will you, dear? Oh, my goodness," she replied vaguely. "Well, I'll try. It's so easy to get these spells confused, when you're out of practice." She touched Sara with the wand.

Sara vanished. In her place, a large pumpkin appeared.

Ryan and Punky and Zender exclaimed in horror. Ryan cried, "What have you done to my sister? Change her back, change her back—"

"Oh, stupid me." The fairy godmother looked at the pumpkin in distress. "I just can't recall how to do that. Shall I turn her into a coach?"

"No," Ryan decided hastily. "Don't do anything

more to her." He heard the hobgoblins quarreling more heatedly with the elves. It sounded as though the game would break up at any minute. "Use that pumpkin over there," he said desperately.

The fairy godmother touched the other pumpkin with her wand. To everyone's relief, a fine golden coach appeared in its place, complete with doors, but no windows.

"Okay, good. Get in, Punky," Ryan said. The smaller boy obeyed, and Ryan shut the coach door behind him. "We'll leave Sara here and try to rescue her later. At least no one's likely to hurt her, as long as she's a pumpkin."

"That's right. Look on the bright side," the fairy godmother smiled.

"Now, fairy godmother, turn me into a coachman," Ryan said.

"I always used white rats for coachmen. Or was it white rats for horses? I'm just not sure—"

From the playing field, several hoarse croaks proclaimed angrily, "I quit! I quit!"

"For gosh sakes, hurry *up*," Ryan told the fairy godmother frantically.

Dithering, she touched him with the wand. Ryan immediately felt weird, different. He was hunched into an unfamiliar position. Not only that, but Zender suddenly loomed over him, much taller than he was. The fairy godmother was like a giantess.

Ryan glanced down at himself with dread, and lifted

a hand to examine it closely. It was not a hand any-more. It was a white paw, with claws.

The frightful truth struck him. He was a white rat. He opened his mouth to protest to the fairy god-mother, but no words came out, only squeaks.

"Oh, I *am* sorry," the fairy godmother said apolo-getically. "I'm just not myself today."

That goes for a lot of us, Ryan thought grimly, nose twitching.

"We'll never be able to pull that coach," Zender said in an undertone to Ryan. "And I don't want to start her working on horses. Everything's bad enough al-ready."

Ryan squeaked in agreement.

"I have a genie friend who lives near here." Zender spoke rapidly, as a couple of hobgoblins bounded into the garden from the playing field. "He has a magic carpet. Maybe he'll lend it to us."

Again Ryan squeaked in agreement, keeping an eye on the hobgoblins. He was appalled to see how huge they looked, now that he had become so small, and close up like this, their faces were hideous.

But to his relief, they paid no attention to him, or to the golden coach, or to the pumpkin who was Sara. They brushed rudely past the fairy godmother, croak-ing complaints to each other about Gorth and the blindfold. They went off to another part of the garden.

Zender dashed away. He returned shortly, pushing a rolled-up carpet. "It's heavy," he panted. He unrolled it; it had an exotic Turkish pattern. "There. I'll get Punky." He ran over to the coach, managed to get the door open, and came back with Punky, who was crying.

"What's wrong, dear?" the fairy godmother asked him tenderly.

"You keep away from me," Punky bellowed loudly between sobs. "You turned one of my friends into a rat and one—"

The hobgoblins scampered into view again, attracted by his loud voice. "That looks like a human boy!" one of them croaked. "Get some stones! Get some stones!"

"Quick! Onto the carpet!" Zender piped. He jumped on himself. So did Punky and the white rat who was Ryan. The carpet wobbled unsteadily up into the air.

"Good-bye!" the fairy godmother called sweetly after it, waving. "Have a lovely trip!"

The hobgoblins seized some stones and hurled them up, cursing. They missed the carpet; it was pretty high already. It was still wobbling a lot. Ryan had to dig in with his claws to keep from falling off. Punky lay on his stomach, clutching the carpet's sides.

Zender got a grip on the fringe. "I don't really know how to steer this," he muttered. His timid face was mushroom-pale.

Punky began to bawl.

"Don't cry. I'm getting the hang of it," poor Zender assured him.

Ryan wished he could tell Punky to shut up. The Wizard of the Wind might be drifting around anywhere. A swift and silent flight to the cavern was their best bet.

Luckily, Punky seemed to realize this. Or maybe he was too scared to speak again. He clung to the carpet and said nothing, as it lurched above the yellow-brick road.

"Most of the wizards live up this road," Zender said softly. "The cavern is near the end of it."

They passed over the gingerbread house, and a thatched cottage, and a house made in the shape of a shoe. They passed above some fire-breathing dragons. From this height, the dragons looked like mere lizards, but Ryan was glad not to be on the ground with them.

He began to enjoy the ride. It was getting smoother; they were going straighter. Zender really *was* getting the hang of it.

At length, the road dwindled to a path. With some swooping trials and errors, Zender brought them down. The carpet landed bumpily on the ground, near a narrow cleft in some rocks.

"This is it," the elf said tensely. "The cavern is in there, Ryan."

Ryan darted into the cavern. Punky and Zender remained outside on the grounded carpet.

Inside, the air was still, like the calm before a storm. It must always be like this when the Wizard was away, Ryan thought. The stillness was uncomfortable, threatening. What a cold, dark, unfriendly place. . . .

Some light came in from the cleft in the rocks, but not much. At first Ryan could see nothing ahead of him but a yawning blackness. He scampered forward, his rat heart pounding with fear.

Then his eyes began to grow accustomed to the dark. He saw, in a niche of rock, a little rainbow of color, with a clear crystal at its center. The crystal shone like a star, and the rays of color moved and shimmered around it.

The magic jewel! Ryan would have laughed for joy, if he could have.

He bounded forward, grabbed the jewel in his mouth, and scurried outside again.

Punky's chubby face broke into a wide grin. "Wa-hoo!" he yelled. "He's got the magic jewel!"

Again Ryan longed to tell Punky to keep quiet, but it was too late. As the carpet rose in the air again, an angry howl of wind rushed toward them.

Chapter

12

THEY TILTED UP CRAZILY, into an increasing gale. Zender tried desperately to steer. He pulled the fringe from one direction to another, and for a minute they were able to fly straight.

"It's the Wizard, isn't it?" Punky asked, in a small scared voice. "He heard me, and he's trying to get us."

"Yes," Zender replied briefly. "He's still a way off, though. He starts the winds going ahead of him. If we can bypass the worst of them—"

Again they were caught by a rushing blast of air. Again the carpet tilted and fluttered. Ryan was in danger of falling off. He dug his claws deeper into it. Punky was on his stomach again, gripping the sides of the carpet for dear life.

Zender gave a tremendous yank on the fringe. Again the carpet changed direction suddenly, and again they got out of the mainstream of wind. Peering down, the jewel tight in his teeth, Ryan saw that they were sailing over the stone wall, out of the kingdom.

A patch of darkness came into the sky, still distant, but growing. "There he is," Zender said. "And if he gets to us himself, we'll be—"

He did not finish, and Ryan was glad not to hear the fatal words spoken. He shut his eyes, not wanting to see the terrible bat-like form approaching.

He could not resist looking again in a moment. The black figure was closer, ever closer. The sky was growing darker and darker. Storm clouds, buffeted by the wind, blotted out most of the sunshine.

Now they were over the woods, the carpet swinging and swaying, but making fair speed.

"Are we almost to the campsite?" Punky asked faintly.

Zender did not answer. His little face was tight with anxiety. He kept struggling with the fringe, trying to guess where the worst of the wind would blow from next.

And still the Wizard kept coming, and the storm blew more fiercely.

Just as Ryan thought they would surely be capsized, or that he would die of fright, he saw the tents below, just ahead. Tracy and some of the others were by the campfire, looking up at the stormy sky.

Now what? he wondered wildly. How could he get the magic jewel back to the Prince in time to save himself and the others from the Wizard's fury?

"Tracy," Punky shouted through the gale. "Get the tank! Get the tank!"

For a stunned moment, Tracy stared up at the magic carpet. Then she ran into Dr. Murk's tent, and was out again in no time, carrying the tank with the flounder in it.

The wind roared, shrieked, howled. The carpet shook as though a giant hand were yanking it around. The sky went almost completely dark; the Wizard was nearly upon them.

They were just over Tracy now. Ryan clamped his teeth firmly on the jewel. The tank looked as big as a swimming pool to him, and the flounder as large as a shark. But he did not hesitate, frightened though he was.

He jumped off the carpet and fell down, down, down. He hit the water in the tank with a big splash, and came against a rough scaly skin. He spat the jewel at the flounder.

A miracle took place. The tank shattered into a thousand pieces and fell to the ground. Instead of a beached flounder, a handsome Prince stood by the campfire.

He was small, smaller than Tracy, a perfect fairy-tale size. In one hand he held the magic jewel.

He smiled at Tracy and at the dumbstruck scientists who were watching. To the white rat at his feet, he said gently, "You must be a human boy, for you've broken the spell."

Ryan nodded.

"Return to yourself, boy," the Prince said.

Ryan became a boy again. He felt sunshine on his face, and looked up at the sky. A small, crumpled, bat-like form was up there, flying harmlessly around the magic carpet. The wind was gone; hardly a leaf stirred anywhere.

"The wicked Wizard has lost his power," the Prince said.

The magic carpet, with Punky and Zender on it, floated peacefully to earth.

"Now I will find my Llura." The Prince strode joyfully to the cove, holding the jewel high. Everyone followed him. At the waterline, he called Llura's name in his mellow voice.

A dolphin swam off to get her. She must be asleep still, Ryan thought. It's early in the morning for her.

But how swiftly she came swimming into the cove! She looked radiantly happy. Mer Blossom was close behind her, also jubilant.

Llura swam closer and closer to the waterline. When she had almost reached the beach, she wriggled, as though she felt a difference in her body. Uncertainly, she stood up. Instead of scales, she wore a dress covered with diamonds. Her seaweed hair was regular hair, blonde and long and fine. She walked into her Prince's arms on a pair of small, shapely feet, in silver slippers.

The Prince kissed her. "Will you marry me, and come live in my castle?" he asked her. "We'll live happily ever after."

"Yes, I will," she said.

The Prince turned to Mer Blossom. "You have always been our faithful friend. Would you like to be a landling too?"

Mer Blossom thought for a moment, swimming slowly. At last she shook her head. "Thank you, no.

I'm a mer-person through and through. I want to stay here, in the sea."

"Oh you do, do you?" Dr. Murk burst out. Ryan had not been thinking about Dr. Murk or noticing him. Now he saw that the old scientist was in a rage.

"First this woman—" Dr. Murk shook his fist at Tracy, "this woman steals my flounder. Then this interfering boy turns him into a Prince. Now the Prince is going around changing mermaids into landlings."

The old man's face was red with fury. He shouted, "I'm not going to be cheated of the glory of this expedition. I'm going to take specimens back, as I planned—"

"Good-bye," Zender said hastily. Before Ryan could thank him for all he had done, the little elf raced off into the woods.

"I'm going to catch a mermaid," Dr. Murk vowed furiously. "*That* mermaid." He pointed at Mer Blossom.

"No, you mustn't do that," Professor Finney spoke up suddenly.

Ryan looked at him with a good, glad feeling. He had not been sure which side his father would be on. Professor Finney looked dazed—who would not be, with a magic carpet and a Prince and an elf and mermaids all coming at once?—but very definite. "That would be wrong."

Tracy smiled. Hepzibah, standing a little apart from everyone else, scowled.

Dr. Murk broke away from the group and made for the dock. With surprising speed for one of his years, he picked up a large seine net and jumped into a boat. The boat had an outboard motor on it. In a trice, he was speeding over the water toward Mer Blossom.

Mer Blossom swam slowly when she felt like it. But she could streak through the sea when she wanted to. She swam well ahead of the boat, leading Dr. Murk farther and farther out.

Near the reefs, she put on a final burst of speed. Then she climbed up on a rock. They were so far away that Ryan could not be certain, but he thought he heard her singing.

Did the singing fascinate Dr. Murk as it had so many other sailors, and cause him to lose his judgment? Or was he just going too fast—and too angrily—to be able to stop in time?

No one would ever know. The speeding boat, aimed at the rock, kept going—and crashed. Dr. Murk was tossed overboard. Pieces of boat flew in the air and scattered over the water.

Mer Blossom watched for a moment. Then she dove off the rock, and swam slowly out to sea.

There were shocked exclamations from the scientists. Professor Finney immediately followed in another boat, to try to rescue Dr. Murk. But everyone knew it was too far, and too late. The old scientist had gone down under the waves.

Tracy asked the Prince, "Can't you save him with the magic jewel?"

"I'm sorry," the Prince said, "but I don't want to save a man who was trying to capture a mermaid."

Everyone fell silent. Professor Finney returned and shook his head.

They all stood silently on the beach, until the ghost ship came sailing into the cove.

"Now for the wedding," Hepzibah purred, yellow eyes glinting.

"What wedding?" the Prince asked, his arm around Llura.

Ryan spoke boldly. He had gone through so much already today that he felt he had nothing to lose. "My father's going to marry Hepzibah, and I wish he wasn't."

The Prince clucked sympathetically. "So that's it. You're up to your old tricks, are you, Hepzibah?" He waved his hand. "Be off with you! I won't let you torment the boy who made my dreams come true."

There was a hiss, a clawing in the air.

Where Hepzibah had been, a black cat stood, eyes blazing. Its tail lashed, and kept lashing in a temper, while the ghost ship came in.

Tracy turned a cartwheel in the sand.

The ghost ship docked. The black-browed ghost captain lowered the gangplank, his parrot on his shoulder.

"No need of your services!" Tracy called cheerfully. "Wedding's been called off."

"You can marry my darling Llura and me instead," the Prince suggested.

The captain came ashore. He married the loving couple in a short ceremony. At the end, the parrot squawked, "Congratulations!"

The Prince said to the captain, "This is the happiest day of my life. I want to make others happy too. What can I do for you?"

The captain replied promptly, "Keep me off that bloomin' ship, sir. I'm everlastin' sick of it."

"I have an idea, sweetheart," Llura told her new husband. "Why not let him come and haunt the castle? He'd be comfortable there. And when we have children, I'm sure they'd love the parrot."

The captain's face broke into a rare smile. "Children . . . I like children."

With a pang, Ryan thought of Sara. "I have something awfully important to ask you." He told the Prince what had happened to his sister.

"And you want me to give her back to you. Of course I will," the Prince assured him. He said to the grownups, "Llura and I are going to take the children into my kingdom, just for a little while."

The ghost captain and his parrot went along too. The Prince led them all directly to the gate. When the dragons saw the Prince, they stopped breathing fire, and moved respectfully aside. No hobgoblin dared throw a stone; they only glared out from behind bushes.

116

Ryan showed the Prince to the place in the garden where they had met the fairy godmother. She had gone, but the golden coach was there. So was the large pumpkin who was Sara, unharmed.

"Return to yourself, human girl." A rainbow of colored light danced from the jewel in the Prince's hand. To Ryan's infinite joy, Sara suddenly stood before them. She and Ryan hugged each other. She began to ask a thousand questions about Ryan's quest for the magic jewel, and he began to answer her.

The ghost captain interrupted. With a trembling finger, he pointed to the gingerbread children and the gingerbread woman, who stood before the gingerbread house on the yellow-brick road. Tears filled his eyes. "Why, it's—it's—"

Only Llura understood immediately. She asked, "Are those your children? And is that your wife?"

He nodded, swallowing. Tears ran down his seamed cheeks.

"So that's it. We heard they had met with an accident on the island, but we didn't know the old witch had gotten them," Llura sighed. "Darling, couldn't you—"

"Of course." The Prince raised his hand. The magic jewel burned with its rainbow colors. The gingerbread children yawned, and stretched, and became human children. The gingerbread woman patted her hair in confusion, looking about her.

The captain ran to them. Their amazement and delight made Ryan feel happy too.

"They'll all be welcome at the castle," Llura said.

Ryan thought admiringly that she really *was* going to be as nice as Snow White, or Sleeping Beauty, or any of the rest of them.

"You children must return now, to your own families." The Prince smiled. "We'll always be grateful to you."

"Thank you," Ryan said.

"Tomorrow," the Prince went on, "the other members of your expedition will have forgotten everything that happened here on the island, except Dr. Murk's death. They will think of that as an ordinary boating accident. Only you children will remember the mermaids."

"I'm glad you're going to let us remember," Sara said.

"Me too," Punky agreed.

"For a while," the Prince smiled again. "Just for a while."

Everything happened as he said it would. The scientists decided to put an end to the expedition and return home. They believed they had not found anything here, and were not likely to. They were eager to get on to another job.

Even Tracy forgot. Later, when she developed pictures of the mushrooms and Gorth's shoe, she could not imagine what they were.

Of the three children, Ryan remembered longest. Gradually he came to realize that the island was not as different from other places as he had supposed. Everywhere, people wanted love and freedom and power. There were some selfish ones who did not care who they hurt in their search for these things. But there were some, too, with nobility of spirit, who wanted to help and share and give.

He learned that too much ambition can destroy a person, on the island or off it. And that life is full of strange reversals: today's flounder may be tomorrow's prince.

One of the best things he learned was that magic does not have to depend on wands or jewels. It can be an enchantment inside people.

His father married Tracy. Sometimes when Ryan sees her turning cartwheels before breakfast, he feels as though all the magic in the world has come to stay, right in his own house.

ELIZABETH STARR HILL is the author of a number of children's books, including *Evan's Corner,* an A.L.A. Notable Book. A dancer, actress, and painter at various times in her life, Mrs. Hill has traveled even more than the Finney children in this story, accompanying her engineer husband to different parts of the world.

They now live in Princeton, New Jersey, but also have a country house "with acres of woods. Foxes, deer, chipmunks, raccoons, and rabbits are our daily companions there. I love to follow a track—or a whim —to catch glimpses of the wild creatures. One day while I was looking at what seemed to be woodchuck holes, Gorth and Zender popped out instead, and this book was born."